A MEDIUM LIFE

THE HAUNTED LIFE COZY MYSTERY SERIES

LYNN CAHOON

A MEDIUM LIFE

A Haunted Life Cozy Mystery series
Book 3

Eddie Cayce was on the edge of setting up her new life in Seattle - including marriage, kids, and a house with a white picket fence. Instead, she found out that her almost fiancé was cheating on her, so she quit her design job over one too many how-to-run-a-copier trainings and moved back home to New Orleans to bury her grandmother.

She didn't expect to inherit not only money, but also her grandmother's powers. Powers that extended her own abilities to see and talk to the dead. A gift that had been mostly dormant in chilly Seattle came roaring back as soon as the ceremony was performed at the reading of the will. Eddie would like to say she's settled back in New Orleans, but there's some issues.

Like the fact her aunt is threatening to make her life miserable until she gives her the power. And a new neighbor that is mysterious as well as being not quite human. Now Eddie needs to make sure she's protected as she builds her new life. And maybe decide which man she's going to date sooner than later. And find out who exactly is Alexander Morgan and the Charming Homes Corporation?

1

My kitchen smells like a mix of fresh baked blueberry muffins and wet dog. Dr. Dexter, my Keeshond puppy must have been outside already, playing in the New Orleans morning rain. Lilac Hooper, my newest employee and house guest, had been up early testing out a new recipe. The girl who had been homeless a few months ago had blossomed after I'd brought her onto the staff team of Cayce's Treasures. Well, technically, she worked under the Goldstein's Antiques section, but I was training her in both sections of the business. The home design department currently only lists Heather King and I as employees. The others, including Lilac, worked for the retail antique store department. My new accountant had explained the division to me several times, but I thought it was overkill. At least for now.

I'm Eddie Cayce. Owner of Cayce's Treasure, Goldstein's Antiques, and this beautiful townhome where we were currently. I'd bought the place for two reasons, okay, maybe three. It was perfect. Three bedrooms, an upgraded kitchen, luxury vinyl plank flooring in most of the rooms, and a working fireplace both in the living room and upstairs in the primary bedroom. Did I mention it had a fenced back-yard, deck, and a one-car garage?

Reason two, it was near the streetcar line and easy for me to get into work at my shop on Royal Street.

And reason three, the place was warded so I didn't see ghosts while I was on the property. The normal security was strong enough to keep my Aunt Franny away as well, which helped keep me safe.

What can I say, family is hard.

Yeah, that's the other thing about me, besides being named for a deceased famous relative, Edward Cayce. I can talk to the dead. I'm called a medium but it's not like those guys you see on television. I have actual conversations with ghosts. Like Harry, the ghost that used to own my antique store. And well, there are always others.

"Good morning, Lilac. Blueberry muffins today?" I sat down and opened my planner, looking at today's always too full list of things to do.

Lilac brought me a cup of coffee. "Since I have the day off, I thought I'd take some over to meet up with Skye. She's so skinny, I think she's not eating enough."

Skye was one of Lilac's friends. They'd bonded during her time on the streets. I didn't quite understand that time of her life, but I knew she tried to make it normal. I hadn't met Skye yet, but from what Lilac said about her, she seemed nice. "How's she doing?"

"Good. She's been staying at the shelter, and I think her case manager has found her an apartment. Or at least a room somewhere. Skye wasn't sure when she called me on Saturday." Lilac turned to the oven and took the muffins out to cool on the granite counter. Then she turned off the oven and the buzzer.

Dr. Dexter smelled the muffins and put his feet up on the counter edge. "Oh, no you don't," I reached over and gently pushed him down. "No sweets for you. You're already so active, I can't even imagine you on sugar."

He barked at me, then continued staring at the place where all the good smells came from.

"Well, at least Dr. Dexter likes the smell of this recipe." Lilac leaned on the counter, sipping her coffee. "Annamae said it was your mom's."

Annamae had worked for our family for years and still was housekeeper, chef, and personal assistant for my brother, Nic Ardronic. Yes, he's the CEO for Ardronic Enterprises and in charge of the family trust. A position that doesn't set well with our aunts and uncles. Worse, when Grandma Andrews died last year, she'd divided her financial estate between Nic and me. Also, she'd passed on a different gift to me, her power to see ghosts. I'd already been dealing with my own talent, and by dealing with it, I meant ignoring it. When Nic did the ceremony at the lawyer's office to transfer Grandma's powers to me, my talent went from someone playing little league to spiking up to the levels in the Hall of Fame. To use a baseball analogy. Anyway, we got the inheritance, monetary and supernatural, and our relatives got nothing. So, they're furious.

"Mom used to bake most mornings." I smiled at Lilac as she watched my reaction. She worried a lot about overstepping her role in my house. I just wanted the girl to be safe and have somewhere she could finish growing up. The world was a hard place. Lilac just needed somewhere she felt comfortable calling home.

Besides, I liked having her around.

"Someone is over at the other condo this morning cleaning. I saw them there while I was waiting for Dex to come back inside." She sipped her coffee. "Do you think Alexander Morgan is arriving soon?"

I didn't know much about my neighbor, except for the fact that he worked for the same corporation, Charming Homes Corporation, that had built and later, sold me my townhouse. And that must have warded the entire building. I wasn't sure what Mr. Morgan did for a living, but I was pretty sure he didn't work for a run of the mill international real estate agency. I'd only met him once, the night of my housewarming party. He came by to meet me while I was trying to reconnect with my parent's friends and allies. We needed people we could count on, especially if the elder members of the family decided to form a coup against us. "I haven't heard anything. Maybe the cleaners just come periodically?"

"That could be true. Anyway, I better get going. I want to take Skye shopping for some house stuff today." Lilac leaned down and gave the dog a belly rub. "I can't take you today, I'm going to be going inside shops and they don't always love pups as much as I do."

I smiled at the exchange between human and canine. Lilac had fallen in love with my dog from the day Bubba had given him to me. Glancing at the clock, I hurried over and fixed me a coffee to go. "I've got to get to work. Wrap up one of those muffins and I'll eat when I get to the store."

"Any plans for tonight?" Lilac asked as she wrapped two muffins, then put them in a baggie for me. "You might want to share."

"Thanks. I'll be home about six if not earlier. I want to work on some rough design plans for the Claiborne Estate redesign. Heather and I are going over tomorrow to measure out the place and walk through the mansion. So these will just be from the county building plans I got last week. Who knows if they've done massive remodeling or not, but I need somewhere to start." My mind was already filled with possibilities for the old home.

"Okay, I'll cook tonight. I should beat you home." Lilac opened the fridge. "Chicken Marsala?"

"Sounds perfect." I slipped on a light jacket and tucked the muffin into my tote. Then I grabbed my coffee.

"You say that every time I tell you what I'm cooking." Lilac held on to Dr. Dexter's collar. He had a habit of trying to sneak out of house when I left in the mornings. "I think you're just trying to make me feel useful around here."

"You *are* useful around here." I turned as I headed to the front door and grinned at her. "Besides, any night I don't have to cook for myself is a perfect night. See you later."

As I hurried down the street toward the cross street where I'd be able to catch a streetcar going into town, I noticed the cleaning car sitting in front of the other side of the house. Maybe we *were* going to get an impromptu visit from our neighbor this week.

Alexander Morgan was tall, handsome, and something else I couldn't quite put my finger on yet. That being said, I wasn't quite sure that he wasn't exactly human. A grey woman stood near the sidewalk watching the house. The ghost turned to me and shook her head. "He's coming back."

"Do you know Alexander?" Talking to ghosts was fairly unreliable, especially ones that looked like they'd been here for quite a while. But like I said, I was curious about my neighbor.

The ghost looked at me like I'd just appeared in her vision. "He's seeking something."

I was about to ask her what when a car drove down the street and the ghost vanished. I continued my trek toward the streetcar stop. "Well, that was less than helpful."

When I got on the trolley, it was nearly empty. My street's stop was near the end of the line, so as we headed back into town, the car would fill up with people heading into work. As I sat, I could still see the house down the street. The ghost had reappeared and had returned to watching the house.

I wrote down a note in my planner to have Mel do some research on the street to see if there had been any deaths near or around my condo. I liked to know who I was chatting with. Especially if they are dead.

When we reached my stop, I still had several blocks to walk to get to my antique shop down Royal Street. I'd bought the shop last year when I'd arrived home after my failed attempt to live a normal life in Seattle. The nearly constant rain and dreary weather hadn't sent me home. No, it had taken a boring career, a failed engagement, and the death of my beloved grandmother before I'd given in and came home to New Orleans.

Now if my brother had his way, I'd be living at the family compound outside the city where Annamae cooked my meals and Nic could keep an eye on me. As it was, he kept close and if he wasn't able to check in, he sent one of his corporate security guys. That's how I met Bubba, or don't call me Beauregard, King. And, his mother, Heather, who now worked with me as a designer.

As my shop came into view, I saw my brother's car parked outside, waiting for me. He opened the door as I approached, finishing a call as he got out of the vehicle. My brother never wasted a minute of time. "Good morning, sister. How was your weekend?"

"Calm. I read while Dr. Dexter played in the yard and dug up the bulbs that Lilac had just planted. How was your trip to California?" I dug for my keys and when I pulled them out, he reached for them. I dropped them in his hand and he unlocked the door. Inside, I keyed in the alarm code and turned on the lights, then held my hand out for my keys, dropping them back into a side pocket in my tote. A place for everything. Since he hadn't answered, I added, "When is Esmerelda coming home for a visit?"

"As the Magic Eight ball would say, 'That is uncertain at this time.' She still feels like that little town needs her." He smiled as he picked up a statue that had been placed on an end table. "She said to tell you hi."

"You really should marry her. She'd keep the family in line." I shut and relocked the door. We didn't open until ten on Mondays. Mel would be arriving soon, and we'd have a short planning meeting for the week before staff arrived. I nodded to the back of the shop where the break room was located. "Do you want some coffee? I have an extra muffin that Lilac put in my bag."

"That would be nice. I left the house before breakfast today. Annamae won't be happy with me when she finds me gone." He held out his arm, indicating he'd follow me.

Harry, the building ghost was hanging near the dining room sets, watching us. "Good morning, Eddie. Nice to see you Mr. Ardronic."

Nic nodded to the ghost. He had the power as well, just not as intense as mine. "Harry, haven't I asked you to call me Nic?"

"Of course, I'm just being polite." Harry floated over toward the window. "It's too bad that the city allowed building behind us. We used to get the most marvelous sunrises. I think I'll head to the roof to check on the weather."

And with that, the ghost disappeared. Nic opened the door to the break room and sat at the table while I made a pot of coffee. We'd go through at least three pots by the end of the day. After it was brewing, I sat down and watched my brother scroll through his emails on his phone. I took the muffins out of the plastic bag and handed him one with a napkin. "Are you just checking in? Or is something wrong?"

He sat his phone down. "There's talk that Uncle Arthur is planning on addressing the board on Friday."

"Something that hasn't been officially run by you?" My father had trained us both in board politics when we reached high school age. The board met annually and basically listened to the report on the state of the business and took their bonus check and left. Oh, and there was a big dinner. All agenda items were run through the CEO, which was Nic.

"I haven't heard anything about a new agenda item. I think he's making his power play. Can I count on your vote?" Nic broke the muffin open. He took a bite and surprise covered his face. "These are like Mom's."

"Lilac got the recipe from Annamae. And of course, you can count on my vote. I was planning on attending the meeting anyway. Since I'm now in town, I decided I needed to be there." I checked the coffee pot and it had finished brewing. I stood and poured us both a cup. We both drank our coffee black so I didn't have to mess with anything else. "You really don't think he's going to try to oust you."

"Yes, I do. There was an incident at one of the fortune telling shops. A break in. Money was taken. Uncle Arthur says it was because we are now allowing our managers to make deposits rather than having a collector each night. He feels like our security standards have loosened." Nic sipped his coffee. "In a way, he's right. But sometimes you have to trust the people who work for you."

"You did the right thing. I remember when Uncle Arthur used to run the collectors. They were a scary bunch. I even felt like I was being threatened when they came to collect. I didn't even handle the money in the shop." I hadn't thought about my summer job at the fortune tellers shop for years. Dad had made it a condition before he'd pay for my college tuition and room and board. Each summer, Nic and I, came home to New Orleans and worked at one of our retail stores. It hadn't been my favorite job since the ghosts had surrounded me, asking them to talk to relatives who'd shown up at our shop. But I wasn't the teller. I just sold the trinkets and scheduled the 'talent's' appointments. I didn't know if those fortune tellers had power or not, but I did get a lot of complaining from the ghosts who came in with their still living relatives for a reading. I pushed back those memories and turned back to Nic. "We have our supporters in line, right?"

"Everyone who was at your open house says they're with us. But you never know until the last vote is cast. We can't let Uncle Arthur take over the company. All the steps I've made to run a clean business will be thrown out the window. And when the hammer falls, we'll be held accountable for his bad deeds." His phone went off. "Speak of the devil."

He walked out of the breakroom to take the call. I took my planner out of my tote and using a highlighter blocked out the time for the board meeting as well as the dinner that night. I wasn't going to let anyone take the company from my brother. Even if it meant a confrontation with my Aunt Franny who would be at the meeting.

As I reviewed my week, I made notes on my daily pages. It was crazy busy, even not counting the hours I was going to have to waste at the board meeting. Those things were horribly boring. But I'd promised Nic I'd be there. Esmeralda should be here, holding his hand as he went through this. However, she was in sunny California. Hiding, just like I had in Seattle. But since Esmeralda wasn't an Ardronic, she could get away with it. I finished my muffin and refilled my cup. Still no Nic.

Finally, I left the break room and went out into the main room. Nic was nowhere to be seen. Mel sat at her desk, working on her computer. I walked over and told her good morning. The I asked, "You haven't seen my brother, have you?"

Mel pointed to the front door. "You just missed him. He walked out and got into that black BMW and drove away. You really need to get a car like that."

I actually *had* a car like that. It belonged to Ardronic Family trust but sat in my garage in case I needed it. In the trunk was a suitcase filled with clothes and a tote bag filled with money. Just in case I had to disappear someday. Nic had insisted on the preparation. The money bag also held paperwork for a new identity. One that the rest of the family would never be able to trace. There was also a gun that I hoped I'd never have to use. I turned back to Mel. "I don't do a lot of driving. Let me grab my tote and we can get started."

I walked back to the break room and texted Nic. *You didn't say goodbye.*

I waited for a minute, watching the little bubbles on my screen. Finally, a response came back. *Sorry. I'm sending Bubba over. 24/7.*

The call hadn't gone well. And worse, Nic thought I needed a full-time bodyguard. I'd have to make sure Bubba's room at the condo was made up. Oh, the joy of being a member of my family. I wasn't sure that my parents or my grandparents had done us any favors when they made us the keeper of the business and the power. Giving us the responsibility had just made us targets for the rest of the family.

I started to put my phone away, then texted one last thought to Nic. *Be safe.*

This time, the response came through quickly. *Always, little sister. Always. And you as well.*

2

I stared at the week on my calendar. Tomorrow, Heather and I were spending the afternoon at the Claiborne Estate. Wednesday, Mel had scheduled me with three interviews for more staff. Thursday, I had an appointment with a new design customer. And Friday, I was with the Ardronic board from nine in the morning until nine at night. I'd gotten a text from Annamae asking if I was staying the weekend at the compound. Probably at Nic's request, but he knew I'd turn him down. Turning down Annamae was harder. But I didn't want to drag Lilac and Dr. Dexter with me, just in case the board had issues. Besides, my house was warded and had just as good of a security system as the compound. And now, I'd have Bubba with me as well.

I turned down the invitation. Saturday, if everything went as planned, I'd be in my home office, happily finishing the designs for the Claiborne Estate so we could get approval to start the project in a few weeks. This was the biggest project I'd taken on since I'd opened my shop here in New Orleans. And if I nailed this one, I'd have tons of new jobs just lining up for the company. If it didn't, well, we could keep fighting, right?

Mel came in and set a bottle of water on my desk. We had bottled water brought in and Mel had bought reusable water bottles with our logo on them. I picked up and opened the bottle, taking a long drink. "Thanks. But I know where the water is located."

"Yes, I know you do, but it's already ten and you haven't had a glass of water all day. If you want to stay hydrated, you need at least eight glasses here at work and two at home." Mel had been working out with a trainer who harped on water consumption constantly. She returned the favor by harassing me and the rest of the staff. She lived alone so we were the only ones besides her friends that she could harangue. "Just say thank you and actually drink."

"I said thank you and took a drink." I adored Mel, but sometimes it was like living with Annamae again. "Hey, let's do a staff lunch next week once this Claiborne Estate thing is in motion. Good or bad, I want to thank everyone for all the hard work."

"We'll just be starting the project," Mel reminded me as she scribbled a note on the pad she carried everywhere.

"I know, but I want this to be a place where we celebrate. Good and bad. Big things and little things. We are going to appreciate each other." I took another drink then set the bottle out of reach on my desk so I wouldn't knock it over. "And seriously, thank you for the water. I do forget when I'm deep in a project."

"Jennifer is downstairs watching the shop so I better get down there too. We're having a contest this month on who can sell more. By item, not by cost, so I might have a chance to win this month." She started out of the office. "Oh, Lilac stopped by. She said Skye's not at the shelter so she's going back to the house and getting Dr. Dexter to walk around the park to see if she can find her."

"Skye is going to drive our Lilac insane. I'm not sure she wants to settle into an apartment and get off the street." I leaned back in my chair and stared out the window.

"Lilac's determined that if she can find her way here, Skye can find a new life as well. I guess they came from similar backgrounds." Mel paused by the door. "And if anyone can get Skye to see a new path, it's our Lilac."

Now that much was true. I knew that Skye had come from a small town in the Midwest like Lilac, but I was sure Skye wasn't special. Lilac could see ghosts, like me. A fact I found out when she was sucked into a conversation, I was having with a ghost here at the shop. She'd talked to Tessa in front of me and outed her abilities. Tessa, the ghost, had found it funny. I figured Lilac was terrified and told her about my own abilities.

It was the first time she'd really trusted me. Now, as Lilac figured out who she was in this new world I'd introduced her to, she'd become stronger and more confident. Now she was on a crusade to save not only Skye, but any young girl who ran away from a situation that wasn't good.

Lilac had a good heart.

~

WHEN I GOT HOME at four, Lilac was already home. I found her in the kitchen, baking cookies. Dr. Dexter laid in the corner, watching for any crumbs that might hit the floor. "I love that my house smells just like my childhood home did when I walked in from school. Cookies and milk. I'd sit at the kitchen table chatting with Annamae about my day, Nic would run in, grab cookies and take off for either the back yard, or later, for some kind of sport practice or game. I swear after he started playing sports, I only saw him at breakfast."

"It must be nice, having a brother. My mom and her boyfriends had a few step kids that would come and go over the years, but no one stayed and none of them were nice." Lilac put another sheet into the oven and sat down at the table. "Do you want something to drink?"

"Water. Sargent Mel is monitoring my intake and I'm failing. I'm supposed to drink two cups tonight." I set my tote on the table and turned to the fridge. "But I can get it. Do we have some of those water bottles from the shop?"

"Of course, we do." Lilac stood and opened a cabinet. "I keep bringing them home and forgetting to take them back. I guess we're going to have to have a back to the shop basket that we can put them in after we wash them."

"I could tuck several into my tote bag. Remind me tomorrow." I took the bottle and filled it. "So this is three cups. If I finish this, I'm good, right?"

"Yep, and I'll even report back to Mel. Maybe she'll stop watching us so closely if we keep hitting her goal." Lilac returned to the table.

"She'll probably just up the goal. Oh, did you find Skye? I should have asked earlier." I sat back down at the table, grabbing one of the peanut butter cookies that Lilac had set on a plate in the middle of the table.

"No, but I heard she might be staying with some guy. I worry about her, but what can you do? I'm not her mom or anything." Lilac lifted her foot on the chair where she was sitting and wrapped her arms around her leg.

I envied her ability to move like that. I wasn't that old, but my days of looking like a pretzel was long gone. Even if I'd started yoga classes with Mel. "You aren't her mom, you're right. But you are a good friend. She'll call you when she needs you."

"Boys drool, girls rule," Lilac chanted the old saying as the doorbell rang. "I'll get it."

I knew who it was. Bubba had dropped me off at the door, then ran home to get a suitcase since his assignment change had been a surprise. And, he had to bring along his cat. Well, I'd kind of insisted on that. If he was staying long term, I wasn't depriving him of Fluffy's company for an extended period. Or I should say deprive Fluffy. The cat loved her owner. Yes, my six foot two, two-hundred-pound bodyguard's cat was named Fluffy. And he teased me about Dr. Dexter's name. The condo was going to be filled with life and energy for the next while. And I liked it like that.

When I heard his voice in the foyer, I went out to greet him and Fluffy. I pointed to the stairs. "You know where your room is. You can set up her cat box in your bathroom. I think I'd give it a while to see how she and Dr. Dexter get along together."

"Sorry about invading your life again. Mr. Ardronic was very clear. I'm, or I guess, we're here for the duration." He nodded to Lilac. "That just means we'll have to have a rematch on that chess game. I don't normally lose."

"Well, get ready to be disappointed again." Lilac leaned down to see Fluffy who was in a cat carrier. "Who's a good kitty?"

"We'll let you get settled. Dinner is at six and Lilac's cooking." I rubbed Dr. Dexter's head as he studied the new housemates.

"I'll get her settled and then walk the grounds. I think I saw someone over at your neighbors." Bubba met my gaze.

"Yeah, rumor is he's gracing us with his presence. Although I guess he doesn't have to announce it. But there's been some bustle over there today." I stared at the connecting wall in the living room and wondered how the other townhouse was arranged.

"I tried looking him up one day at the office. Officially, he barely exists. He has a valid passport and a driver's license from Maine. No arrests. No marriages. Nothing else. He doesn't even own the condo. Charming Homes does." Bubba sounded tenuous. Like Alexander Morgan was a puzzle he hadn't figured out.

"So the townhouse is a corporate perk?" Now that was interesting. What business was Charming Homes in? "Maybe they do houses for people like me with gifts."

"Maybe." Lilac stood from where she'd been crouched with Fluffy. "They do a great job. I'm sleeping great here. Everywhere else, well, I had visitors."

"There would be a market for that kind of specialty housing." Bubba agreed, pulling Lilac into a short hug. Everyone wanted Lilac to feel safe. She was like the little sister you didn't realize you needed. I wondered if that defense mechanism was also part of her talent. One that she hadn't used until she had to run away from home. "For sensitives, like you."

She pushed away from him, laughing. "You're calling me a freak?"

"I would never do that." He looked shocked. "Maybe strange, weird, or just odd. But never a freak."

I gently pushed him toward the stairs. "Okay you two, stop fighting. I'm going to my office to work. You two get along until dinner."

"Yes, ma'am." Bubba grabbed his suitcase, tote bag, and the carrier and headed upstairs.

Lilac bumped her hip into mine. "So Bubba, huh?"

"Nic is concerned about the upcoming board meeting. Bubba's here just as a precaution." I studied Lilac as we walked toward my office. "You should be careful too. If they think they can get to me through you, they'll use it."

"Okay, I won't go hanging out in dark alleys where I can be snatched." She slapped a hand across her forehead. "Except for today. And if Skye calls me to go pick her up, I'll take someone with me."

"That would make me feel better." I opened the door to my office. "All joking aside, the board vote is Friday. So just be careful. We'll talk about this again after they've left town."

"Does anyone but Nic and the people at the shop even know I live here with you?" Lilac paused at the door.

I laughed as I sat down at my desk. "I'm coming to believe my life is under twenty-four seven watch. I think the answer is yes. I'd move you for the week, but I think we're safer here in the townhouse."

AFTER DINNER, someone knocked on the front door. We were in the living room, Lilac and Bubba just starting their chess match. I was reading a book about the history of New Orleans. Dr. Dexter was at my feet. Fluffy had taken up a spot on the back of the couch by Bubba. We looked like a perfect suburban family.

Bubba looked at me and nodded. Then he went to open the door. I pretended to read, but all the hairs on my arms were standing straight up. "May I help you?"

"Good evening, I was wondering if I could have a quick chat with Ms. Cayce. I'm her neighbor, Alexander Morgan." The southern lilt in his voice echoed in the foyer. Odd for a guy from Maine.

I set the book down on the table and met the men at the door. "Good evening, Mr. Morgan. How can I help you?"

Bubba stepped back but didn't leave the foyer.

Alexander smiled at me. "Now, Ms. Cayce, I thought we were past the formal greetings."

"Sorry, Alexander. Why don't you come in?" I felt Bubba stiffen behind me.

Alexander glanced behind me at Bubba and shook his head. "Some other time, perhaps. I just came by to let you know that I'm in town. I didn't want to scare you if you heard noises next door. I also wanted to give you this. I understand you're working on the redesign for the Clayborne Estate. I'm sure you'll find a lot of history in that house. The family was remarkable."

I took the book he held out. It was old and seemed to be a biography of the Clayborne family. "Thank you. I'm not sure how you knew I'd taken the project on, but this will be helpful. There's not a lot about the family that's been published."

He smiled. "I'm sure there's not a lot about the Ardronic or Andrews family in the general book stacks at the library either. You just need to know where to look. Good evening, Eddie."

With that, he turned around and walked back to where the sidewalk coming to my front door divided and then went to his house. Alexander was dressed in an expensive black suit with black leather shoes. If he hadn't been so crazy attractive, he would have looked like a funeral home director. Instead, he looked like a rich businessman who got what he wanted. No matter what.

I just didn't know what he wanted this time. I shut the door and turned back to Bubba. "Well, that was weird."

"A little," he admitted. "Can I check the book? It's not spelled, is it?"

"No, that I would have felt. It's just an old book." I handed it over to Bubba and let him flip through it. "I'm just wondering how he knew I was working on the Clayborne Estate. I didn't announce it. Mel knows and Heather. But no one else here, except the Clayborne representative."

"The book's clean. No messages tucked into the pages." Bubba handed me the book, but he looked troubled.

"But?" I knew he was still thinking.

He shook his head. "I just wish we knew more about Mr. Morgan and what he does. It would make me feel better."

I squeezed his arm as we left the foyer. "You and me both."

THE NEXT MORNING, the three of us were walking to the streetcar stop when I realized Lilac had stopped walking and gone pale. "Did you forget something?"

She stared into the street. Nothing was there as far as I could see. Then she smiled a little and shook her head. "Sorry, no. I just thought I heard something. Someone calling my name."

Since I'd already chatted with a ghost on the street yesterday, I didn't like this turn of events. I stepped closer to Lilac. "Give me your hand. Sometimes touch helps focus the energy."

As Bubba watched the real world, Lilac and I scanned the street for any sign of spirits. There was nothing. I released her hand and met his gaze. "I don't see or hear anyone."

"Me either. At least now. But I could swear, I did hear my name just now." She shivered and pulled her sweater closer.

I looked back toward where we came. A light was on in Alexander's upstairs and for a second, I thought I could see a figure. It disappeared and I turned to Lilac and took her arm. "Do me a favor. I know we're already on high alert due to the board meeting, but can you make sure you're not alone with our neighbor?"

"Do you think he's . . ." Lilac started but I shook my head to stop her from saying anymore.

"I'm not sure what I think, but you hearing someone calling your name, it's a bad sign."

Bubba pointed toward the cross street. "If we don't want to wait around another twenty minutes, we better get moving. The streetcar is almost at our stop."

We arrived just in time to catch the streetcar and we all swiped our cards. I bought several monthly cards for all my employees. Even if they didn't live on the line, it was an easy way for us to go check out new projects or attend sales, as long as they had delivery options.

Bubba sat down next to me watching out the windows toward the house. He lowered his voice to almost a whisper. "What just happened?"

"I'm not sure, but Lilac heard someone calling her. I ran across a ghost at the same spot yesterday talking about our Mr. Morgan. Maybe there's more going on with him than we know." I snuck a quick glance at Lilac but she was staring at her phone, her headphones already plugged in. If I knew her, she was listening to music. But the emotion of what had just happened, hadn't worn off yet. She was worried about something.

"I'll see what I can dig up at the shop." Bubba leaned back as the streetcar started up again after another stop for a woman and her daughter.

When we arrived at the shop, Detective Charles Boone was standing outside, a cup of coffee in one hand and scrolling through his phone on the other. Boone was a friend as well as the detective assigned to the Royal Street area as well as most of the French Quarter.

He watched as we approached, his facial expression unreadable. I knew this wasn't a social call. He tucked his phone away and pulled out something from his jacket pocket. I felt Bubba tense, but it wasn't a gun. It was a plastic bag.

"Hey Boone, what are you doing here this early? Let me open the door and I'll refill that coffee." I pulled out my keys, and unlocked the door, turning off the alarm. Bubba, Lilac and, finally, Boone followed me inside, shutting the door behind him.

"I hate to do this so early, but we have a situation. We found this card on someone this morning." He handed me the plastic bag. It was the Goldstein Antiques business card. My name and number for the shop was listed on the front.

"This is mine. Where did you find it?" I was beginning to believe the sabotage from the board meeting was already starting. I wondered if I needed a lawyer. Bubba was already texting on his phone. I knew he was talking to Nic.

Boone pointed to the card. "Turn it over."

I did. Lilac's name and cell phone number was written on the back. The cell phone I'd supplied for her when she started working and living with me. My gaze flicked to Lilac and I saw Boone's had as well. "You didn't answer me. Where did you find this?"

"In the pockets of a girl we found down by the river. She was attacked. We think her name was Skye." Boone turned to Lilac. "Did you know her?"

Lilac sank into a nearby chair as tears flowed down her face. "It was Skye's voice who spoke with me this morning. She's dead."

3

After Boone had talked to Lilac in the employee break room, I cornered him on his way out. "You don't think she had anything to do with this, right?"

Boone took my arm. "No. And I would tell you if I did. The body was torn to shreds. I don't think Lilac has the strength to do anything like this. No, we're looking for a male, probably about Beauregard's size. Do you know where he was last night around nine?"

I huffed out a laugh. "Actually, I do. And you're not going to like my answer. He was sitting in my living room, playing chess with Lilac. You know he didn't do it. You just like messing with Bubba."

"Maybe. Why was 'Bubba' in your living room last night? Are you two dating?" Boone didn't meet my gaze with this question. He'd asked me out since I'd gotten home, and I'd told him I needed some time.

"No, he was working. Nic thinks the board meeting might get a little messy this week. Bubba's been assigned to watch me for the upcoming future." I touched his arm, trying to ease his discomfort. "I'm not dating anyone. Not yet."

"I know, you're still getting over the cheating fiancé." He shrugged off my hand. "I just wanted to make sure I hadn't missed my chance.

Anyway, you're right, Bubba's not on my short list. I'm talking to the zoo next. Apparently, they have some missing wolves."

"You really think there are wolves hunting humans in New Orleans?" My thoughts turned to Alexander Morgan's reappearance. And now a girl was dead? Was that just coincidence? "It seems unlikely."

"Oh, I'm sure there's probably a very human reason behind this killing. But it doesn't help that there was a full moon last night. I'm getting questions from the press about New Orleans having a were-wolf." His phone went off and he swore as he checked the caller id. He tucked the phone back into his pocket after sending the caller to voice mail. "I've got to go. If Lilac remembers or hears anything about this guy that Skye was staying with, have her call me."

I followed him back out to the showroom and stood next to Mel as he left the building. She turned to me. "Is Lilac all right?"

"I think she's going to need a few days to process. Skye was a close friend and Lilac thought she was getting off the streets to safely. Then this happens. It's a lot to process." I sank into a chair. "Maybe we can have her work on inventory up on level five? Heather and I are due at the mansion in an hour. I don't want Lilac out of the building, alone."

"Is that why Bubba's here?" She nodded to where he was standing with his back against the wall, watching the showroom.

"Actually, no." I filled her in on the board meeting and the possible overthrow of Nic as CEO. "So he's here to watch me. Maybe I should bring Lilac with me today?"

Lilac had walked out of the break room and heard my words. "No, I'm fine. I won't go looking for revenge or anything stupid, I promise. Besides, maybe if I hang around here, Skye might come to talk to me. She's been here before."

"Sometimes when people die, the spirit leaves this plane." I didn't want Lilac to think that her friend might just pop in for a chat.

"But I know that was her calling my name earlier," Lilac insisted. "Maybe she's just trying to build up her ability to talk to the living."

"Maybe. I just don't want you to get your hopes up. And I defi-nitely don't want you wandering down by the river." There, I'd said it.

I knew I didn't have any control over where Lilac went or didn't, but I hoped she'd take the advice as it was offered, as a friend. A friend who was freaking out and acting like her mother.

Lilac let the words sink in. Then she shrugged. "Sounds like good advice to me. Even if it was given with a bit of a parental tone."

Mel choked back a laugh.

"Sorry, I know I overstepped. I'm just worried about you." I saw Lilac smile and realized they were both laughing at me. "Fine, I'm overprotective. Now I know how Nic feels."

Heather King walked in and went over to give her son a kiss on the cheek. "Good morning, Beauregard."

He grimaced. "Good morning, Mom. I'm working here."

"I know, big man with an important job." Heather patted his chest, then walked over to the group. "You all look freaked out. What's going on?"

Mel and Lilac caught Heather up as I ran upstairs for my file on the Clayborne Estate. When I got back, Mel was talking with a customer and Lilac wasn't in sight. Heather stood and pulled out her keys when she saw me approaching. Bubba was right behind me.

"Where's Lilac?" I asked as I tucked the file into my tote with the book Alexander had given me last night. I had several notes and ideas about ways we could renovate without losing the historic charm.

"She's upstairs. Mel gave her a list of items that are supposed to be on the fifth floor." Heather grinned at me. "I think we're not going to need to schedule time doing inventory if we can use Lilac for this."

"We'll see how she is tomorrow. I just wanted her to not have to be on and talking to customers if she's not feeling up to it." I turned to Bubba who'd taken his mother's keys. "I suppose I can't talk you into staying here with her. At least for today."

"No. But I had a better idea because I figured you'd try this. The company is sending over another guy, Danny, who will watch out for Mel, Jennifer, and Lilac. Just during working hours, unless there's a problem. If that happens, we'll probably ask you to close the shop for a few days."

"Having guards around is going to freak out the customers." I sighed as I surveyed my shop filled with antiques and odd pieces.

"The official story that customers will get from the staff is that there have been some break ins on Royal Street. Not here, of course, but other shops. The local police have recommended caution. Now it's all Boone's fault." Bubba grinned as they moved out to the sidewalk.

They drove to the other side of town, on the far side of the Garden District and parked in the cracking driveway of a plantation style house. One that had been left to crumble years ago. The faded white columns had ivy growing up most of the height and there was moss on the siding.

Bubba climbed out. "I thought you were doing an interior design project. This place looks like it needs torn down. Or used for an awesome horror flick. Maybe something with vampires?"

"I assure you, there are no vampires or squatters on the grounds." A woman climbed out of the sports car that had just parked next to Heather's van. "I'm sure there's a few critters around, but we hired an exterminator to come in next week."

I smiled and hurried over to the woman. Eliza Clayborne Summers was my client and the new heir of the estate after her uncle had died. She wore a skirted white suit topped off with a large sunhat. I was certain the suit was designer, but I wasn't sure where she got her hats. The outfits I'd seen her wear all enhanced her assets; a fact Bubba seemed to have noticed as well. "Eliza, so good to see you again. How long are you in New Orleans?"

"I was leaving on Saturday, but I've heard there's a problem with the board meeting Friday so I might not be here as long as I'd thought." She gave me a quick hug as she leaned into whisper, "What's going on with your Uncle?"

I leaned back and looked at her. "Is he vying for your support?"

"He was, now, he seemed to have disappeared. The rumor is he's been running something under the table?" The stare I got from her made me uncomfortable, but I knew she was reading my aura, trying to see what side I was on. She'd already declared Uncle

Arthur to be a problem. Eliza wanted the family corporation to grow and to do that, we needed to run a clean company. Something Uncle Arthur was against. "You'll let me know if there's anything I can do, right?"

"Of course. I'll talk to Nic tonight. This is the first I've heard about a delay in the board meeting." Hopefully, Eliza's intel was true. Nic needed more time to shore up his supporters. "So let's talk about the house."

Eliza walked us through the mansion, talking about her vision for the ancestral family home. The place was quiet, at least from the ghost realm. I wasn't sure if the Clayborne's had warded it or if their relatives had all just passed on peacefully. Heather took notes as we talked and as she and Bubba measured all the rooms, I said goodbye to Eliza. "Thanks for giving me this project. I know it will open a lot of doors for me."

"Eddie, you deserve it. Franny's been bad mouthing you and your brother at the country club for months now. After you finish reviving this monstrosity, you'll have more customers than you can handle. I'll throw a party and introduce you to everyone I know." She gave me a hug. "Franny's just angry about her mother not leaving her the power. We all know that. And we all know that she isn't the right person to have it in the first place."

"Thanks for your support. Nic and I appreciate it." I had a feeling that I was going to have to confront my aunt, again, sooner than later. Her actions were affecting my business. And that I wasn't going to stand for, even from a relative. "I'll get new drawings and project specs back to you before the end of the month."

"I've already sent you the retainer and a generous amount to start the work. I'd love to get this finished before Marsha gets out of school. We could spend the summer in Colorado, then come down here for the winter. Best of both worlds." Eliza kissed me on both cheeks. "I trust your judgement. Just keep me in the loop and don't ask me about color or design choices. I trust you."

I went back inside after watching Eliza get in her car. As I entered the foyer, I noticed a card on the table. Charming Homes. On the back of the card, someone had written a short note. *House warded on February 25th. Contact us for any slippage.*

So not only did Eliza know about Charming Homes, but she'd also used them for the house. I stepped out on the porch to try to stop her from leaving. I needed to ask her some questions about the company. But the blue sports car and it's driver were long gone. "Darn it."

Bubba came out the door and watched me. "Something wrong? Don't tell me you lost the bid. I've been in too many tiny closets here getting measurements for my mom to have that all disappear."

"You're on the clock, why does it matter what you do?" I teased Bubba as I turned around and headed back into the house. "But no, your sacrifices were not in vain. I just realized that Eliza used Charming Homes to ward the place. I wanted to find out what she knew about the company. And maybe, my neighbor."

We worked for a few more hours, getting measurements for the rooms and taking pictures. As I surveyed the attic, I found a stash of old furniture and antiques. "Hey Heather, we need to sort through this and find out if there's anything we can salvage for the restoration."

Heather glanced at her watch. "I'd say I'd stay late but I'm picking up the grandbaby from school today."

"Anyway, we can grab a late lunch?" Bubba brushed cobwebs off his shoulders. "I'm starving."

"Let's go grab lunch, then Heather can drop us off at the shop. Heather, can you get this sorted tomorrow? Do you need help?" I leaned against the doorway in the attic. "I have interviews, but maybe I can send..."

"Don't say me, I'm by your side until your brother sends me back to the corporate offices." Bubba grabbed bottles of water that I'd stuck in a backpack and gave to him before we left the shop. He handed us each one. "Sorry, Mom."

"I wasn't going to say you," I replied as I opened my water. Okay, so I had been going to say Bubba, but he didn't need to know that. "What about Lilac? She's always wanting to get more into the restoration side of the business. I'll send her over with you tomorrow and if Eliza's intel is correct, my Friday just got cleared so we can all come back Friday if you need us."

"We'll have it all ready for demo by the first of the week." Heather clapped her hands together, which didn't really have the affect she wanted since she still held the water. "Oh, that is if you have plans done by then."

"Have the construction team ready to go mid next week." I was glad I'd already started my plans. "We still have to get Eliza's final approval on the plans. Even though she 'trusts' us, I want her to know at least where we're going. I believe we can be ready to start next Wednesday."

Bubba was watching out the attic window. When his mom and I stopped talking, he turned back to us. "So does that mean we're ready to go eat?"

"The guy is a bottomless pit." I nodded and headed down the stairs.

Heather who was following me, agreed. "You should have seen my food bill when I had two of them in high school. They ate like they were professional football players or something."

When we got downstairs, I saw Bubba on his phone, texting. He met my gaze and I could see that something was wrong.

"Let's get this place locked up and get in the car." He headed toward the back door to lock it.

I grabbed my jacket and sketch pad. When he came back through, Heather was hurrying toward the car, but I waited for Bubba since I had a key to the front door to lock it. He shut the door and took my key, locking it. "What's going on?"

"Lunch is going to have to wait. That was the other security guy. Lilac's disappeared." He checked the door, then gave me back my keys and we hurried to the car. As he backed out of the driveway, I put on my seatbelt, then dialed Lilac's cell. No answer.

I called the shop and got Mel. "What's happening?"

"Lilac took off. I thought she was upstairs doing inventory, but when Danny went up to check on her, she was gone." Mel explained. "I'm sorry, I should have kept her closer."

"If she's not at the shop, she's trying to figure out what happened to Skye. I should have realized that Skye was talking to her. She reached out when we were getting on the streetcar this morning."

"You think Skye's ghost is leading Lilac to her killer?" Mel took in a breath that I heard over the phone. "Skye would be putting her in danger."

"Sometimes Lilac doesn't think of those things. Look, we'll be back in thirty minutes." I looked at Bubba who verified my estimate. "Order sandwiches and drinks for all of us. I'm going to figure out where Lilac went before she gets herself in trouble."

After I hung up the phone, Heather leaned forward from the back seat. "How are you going to find out where she went?"

I tucked my phone into my tote. "Hopefully, Harry was listening in on Lilac and Skye's conversation. Sometimes it pays to have a resident ghost in the building."

My phone rang and I reached for it again. I should have just left it out. "Hey, Nic."

"What's going on with you? Are you all right? Your energy is all over the place." As my brother, Nic had a special connection to my thoughts. I tried to keep him out of my head, but even when I succeeded at not letting him into my thoughts, he could feel my emotions. And times like this, that was just as bad.

"Lilac left the shop. She was supposed to be doing inventory, but no one can find her. We think she went to find out what happened to Skye. That's her friend who was killed recently." I paused, thinking about what Eliza had said. "Is there any chance that Ardronic Enterprises was involved in this?"

"Not officially," Nic admitted, "but I believe that Uncle Arthur is courting the homeless population for seers. This friend of Lilac's, did she have power?"

"Lilac didn't say she did, but maybe she was just good at knowing what to say. A lot of mortals are that way. They don't really talk to the dead, but they are good at guessing the next sentence based on your reaction. If I can find Lilac, I'll ask her." I didn't want to ask the next question, but it would be there even if I didn't. "What is Uncle Author doing?"

"He's building his own army." Nic said, confirming my suspicion. "Oh, and due to this killing, the board meeting has been postponed. Most of the out of towners don't want to be in town while the police are investigating the murder of a young girl."

4

When we arrived back at the store, Mel took the three of us back to the employee break room where the food had been delivered. Kirk, our night watchman, was there as well. He stood as soon as I walked in the room. "Mel told me to wait here for you. She said I should eat. I'm sorry, should I have waited for you?"

Kirk was still getting used to being off the street. In fact, most of the day he spent on the streets, trying to get kids into shelters or giving them money to call home if that was an option. He'd brought Lilac to me a few months ago. And now, he was one of our best chances to find her. I sat down and pulled a sandwich and bottle of soda toward me. "Kirk, I'm so glad you're here. Mel was right, we need your help."

He looked around the room and as he did, Bubba and Heather took food as well. It looked like a group of people just having lunch. I hoped the anxiety we felt over Lilac being missing wouldn't agitate Kirk. Bubba sat as far away from Kirk as possible. Kirk didn't like him. Mostly, Kirk called Bubba the big guy and worried that he would call the police to get him arrested. Getting Kirk off the street had been the first step in his start to a more normal life, but it wasn't the last.

"You need my help? Who's in trouble?" Kirk took another bite of his sandwich, then washed it down with several gulps of soda.

"Lilac's not here. We think she went out to find out what happened to her friend, Skye." I wished I had Skye's picture to show him. That might help him focus.

"Skye is gone. The cops showed her picture around yesterday. Someone had seen her body. She's with the angels now." He took another bite of the sandwich.

"Do you know who killed Skye?" Bubba asked, careful not to look at Kirk while he was asking.

Kirk shook his head. "I tried to keep Lilac's friend safe like she'd asked me. But Skye just laughed at me when I told her the man in the cape wasn't good. She said he'd hired her and soon, she'd be able to afford her own place."

"The man in the cape?" I leaned forward, trying to read Kirk's facial features. "Who's the man in the cape?"

"He comes at night. People say he gives them jobs. Pays them money. Sometimes they come back, sometimes not. They have to be able to pretend. Some people can, others not." He looked at me. "Can I have another sandwich?"

"Of course." I moved the plate closer to him and he took a roast beef one from the side. "Kirk, do you know the man in the cape?"

He shook his head while he ate. "He doesn't like me. He says I tell lies about him. But I just warn them. Warning them that some don't come back isn't a lie. I warn them."

I finished my sandwich and waited but Kirk was done talking. Soon, he grabbed his bag and stood.

"Thank you for lunch. I'm going to my room to read." He left the room and went to the door that led to his small apartment in the back.

I looked over at Bubba and Heather. "Either of you get a feel or anything from him? I'm kind of out of ideas."

"I think we need to find the man in the cape." Bubba finished a third sandwich, then pushed his plate away. "After we locate Lilac. Have you tried to trace her phone?"

"I didn't set up the locator app on the phone." I knew Bubba was going to ask why not, but instead, it was Heather who spoke next.

"Lilac's a grown woman. If we think she's in danger later, Eddie can call the phone company since it's her phone. But putting a tracker on it is invasive." Heather picked up her empty plate and Bubba's and threw both in the trash. She covered the rest of the sandwiches with the clear cover that had come from the caterer. "I'll go out front and tell Mel and Jennifer and the other security guard to come back and eat."

"I'm going to find Harry. If he doesn't know where Lilac went, I'll call the phone company." I stood and cleaned off my and Kirk's section of the table. "So we're looking for a man in a cape. Like Jack the Ripper."

"Except he's talked to Kirk before. Told him he was telling lies. He may not be as invisible as Jack the Ripper turned out to be. And he may be gathering people to work for him." Bubba held the door open for me.

"Maybe a pimp?" I asked, afraid of the answer.

"Possible." Bubba followed me to the elevator. "Where will Harry be at this time of day?"

I shrugged. "Hard to say. He shows up when he wants to but he doesn't like being on the sales floor during the day as people are around. Let's start in my office, then we'll go up to where Lilac was working if he's not there."

"I talked to Danny and he said that he saw her working upstairs when he got here at ten thirty. When he went back up an hour later, she wasn't on the floor and the window was open to the fire escape. That's when he called me." Bubba pushed the button for the elevator. "He feels horrible. He can't believe a teenager could dodge him."

"He must not have kids yet. Just wait." I watched as Heather met Mel, then Danny on the floor, pointing them toward the back. Jennifer was still with a customer.

As we walked off the elevator on the third floor where the offices were situated, Harry was waiting for me. He floated outside my doorway, wringing his hands. "Oh, thank God. You're here. You need to hire more people who can see me, like Miss Lilac so I don't have to wait around for one of you to show up to warn everyone."

"I'll add it to my list of hiring criteria. I take it you know where Lilac is?" I didn't bother going into my office, we could have this conversation in the hallway. Bubba had frozen by the wall as soon as he'd decided that I was talking to a ghost.

"When Miss Lilac was working upstairs, she got a visitor. A slight young woman who seemed to be her friend. Miss Lilac called her Skye." Harry shook his head. "The names parents put on their children these days. No wonder everyone's angry and vicious."

"Skye is a pretty name." I replied, but then I saw Bubba's face. Right, there was no use in fighting with a ghost. Especially one that had information you wanted. Bubba could hear and see ghosts, but I think it was only because he was near me. Somehow, he shared my power when we were together. I didn't think that was possible until I'd seen it happening. "Anyway, sorry. What happened then?"

"Miss Skye told Miss Lilac that she needed to go to the rainbow on Piety street. That there would be a package there for her." Harry sighed and the temperature in the room dropped. "I should have stopped her. I was so focused on not letting anyone see I was eavesdropping, I let that poor girl go trasping down to the river all by herself. You know that area isn't the friendliest of places. Or it hadn't been when I was alive."

"Thank you for telling me, Harry. This is very helpful. Before I leave and you disappear, is there anything else I need to know. Anything about Skye that seemed off?" I could see Harry had worked himself up so much that he was starting to fade at the edges. Soon, he'd be off rebuilding his power or whatever it was that kept him here at the shop.

"There's something wrong with the spirit. She seemed heavy." Harry opened his mouth to say more, but then gently vanished.

I turned to Bubba. "How in the world can a spirit be heavy?"

"That's a new one on me. Are we going to find Lilac now?" Bubba held his hand over the elevator button.

I nodded and he pushed the call button. Maybe there was more going on with Lilac's disappearance than met the eye. I'd hate to miss something, just because we thought we knew what we were looking for as we searched.

I found Mel standing in the hallway, eating her sandwich and watching the front door, just in case Heather got overwhelmed. I let her know where we were going and told her we'd call one way or the other when we got to the spot.

She nodded to Danny who was standing by the wall, watching. "Are we keeping him?"

"I think so. There are a lot of moving parts right now, and until I know what's going on, I don't want anyone alone. At least not at work." I paused before I moved to the doorway. "And maybe after work, too."

"My college roommate is in town and staying with me. I won't be alone until after next week when she leaves. Jennifer has her husband and kid. And Heather has her husband too." Mel rattled off the staff's situations to ease my mind.

"And Heather's getting the grandkid tonight as well. Okay, that makes me feel better." I stepped toward the entry way, but Mel's next question stopped me.

"What about you, Bubba? Will you be alone tonight?"

I turned and saw Mel grinning at him. Before he could answer, I filled in the silence. "Bubba is staying over with Lilac and me so I'm not alone."

I knew I must have turned red as I turned back around and marched toward the front door. I could feel Bubba hurrying to catch up.

He caught my arm as we were out on the street. "Hold up. What was that all about?"

"Mel thinking she's match making between the two of us. You've been assigned to watch out for me, that's all." I glanced around to get my bearings.

Bubba pulled me closer and I realized I'd almost stepped in front of a stroller being pushed by a jogging mama. "That's not all, but I'm willing to wait until you know what this is. I don't care how you label it as long as you don't call it a mistake or a misunderstanding. I enjoy spending time with you. I'd do it even if I wasn't being paid. Right now, that is beside the point. We need to go see if we can find Lilac before she gets herself into trouble."

"Harry said the rainbow on Piety street. Any clue to where that might be?" I started walking down Royal Street toward Piety.

"I think I might." He glanced at my shoes. "Good thing you have walking shoes on today."

"We could get a cab," I glanced over at the busy street. Cars were going a lot slower than the walkers were. "But I think we're going to get there faster on foot."

"I agree. Besides, I like a walk during the day. Your house is a little small. At the corporate offices, I take the stairs all day long to stay in shape. Then they have a gym for our use for after work. Sometimes I'm in there every night I'm working. It's a good gym."

"I don't think any gym is good." I fell into pace with Bubba. Not too slow, not to fast, it was a Goldilocks kind of walk – just right. "I'd rather run outside. I like being one with nature."

Bubba picked up an empty plastic cup and put it into a trash can. "I'm not sure you can call this nature."

"If you run early, you miss the people. And if you run after the street sweepers have gone through the area, you miss the trash too." We walked around a group of tourists who were planning where to have an early dinner. "I hope what Mel said didn't upset you. I know you're just doing your job."

"Am I just doing a job?" Bubba looked over at me while we waited for the streetlight to change. "I guess I thought you knew I was interested in being more than just your bodyguard. I thought we were at least, friends. But if I'm misreading the signals, I apologize."

"No, I mean, yes, we're friends." Now I felt like an idiot bringing it up. "I just don't want you to think I expect something else."

He tried to squash a smile. "Oh, dear, are you trying to proposition me?"

I felt my eyes go wide but before I could answer, he took my arm and drug me across the street.

"I'm kidding. I know you're just out of a relationship that ended badly. The next step is on you. I've told you I'm interested, but I'm not going to push it. If we stay in the friends zone, it happens. If not, that's good too." He nodded toward the large iron pedestrians bridge in front of us. "That's where Harry said to go. Do you see her?"

The bridge was busy with people crossing over to the park that ran next to the Mississippi River. It was a good place to walk and think or meet up with friends. Or just sit at a table soaking up the sunshine if you had nowhere else to go. "I don't. Do you see her?"

We stood together on the sidewalk, scanning the area. Finally, Bubba grabbed my arm and pointed to the top of the bridge. "There."

Lilac and Kirk were walking over the bridge and toward us. When she saw us standing there, her face turned white. She said something to Kirk and pointed to us. When they reached the bottom, I pulled Lilac into a hug. "Are you all right?"

"I'm fine. What's going on?" She looked back and forth between Bubba and me.

Now I wanted to slug her. Or stamp my feet. I'd been so worried and she was acting like I was the crazy one. "You were told to stay in the shop with a security guard. You left to try to find out what happened to Skye. You could have been killed yourself."

Kirk held up his hand. "After lunch, I called one of my friends and he said he saw Lilac here. I came to find her."

"I'm sorry, Eddie. Skye said she was waiting for me here. Waiting to talk to me." Lilac's shoulders dropped. "But she wasn't. Then Kirk found me and we were heading back to the shop. I didn't think I was gone that long."

"Lilac, you don't understand what's going on here. I don't think Skye was the one who reached out to you." I smiled as Kirk side-stepped around to be on the other side of me from Bubba. "And if something had happened, I would have felt horrible for leaving you at the shop today."

"What do you mean?" Lilac looked around the bridge. "You think another ghost told me to come here?"

I put my arm on her shoulder. "I think we need to go back to the shop before we discuss this."

Kirk told us he had a few stops to make before he headed to his apartment, so we parted ways. As he walked away, Lilac looked up at me. "It was nice of him to come find me."

"I know. He's a good guy." I watched as he greeted a homeless man who was sitting on the sidewalk by a building. He slipped the man some money as they talked. "He really cares about people."

As we crossed the street, a cold wind blew off the river and I shivered. I looked back toward the bridge and Alexander Morgan stood there, watching us leave. I froze in place, wondering what he was doing there.

Bubba turned around, sensing that I'd stopped. He put a hand on my back and I looked up at him. "Are you okay?"

I turned back and pointed toward the bridge and Morgan, but no one was there. I scanned the area and couldn't find him. Was Alexander Morgan the one who lured Lilac to the riverside park? "I thought I saw someone. But I guess I was wrong."

5

I'd planned on visiting my neighbor to see what game he was playing when I got back to the condo. The more I thought about what I'd seen at the bridge, the more I was convinced that I had seen Alexander Morgan that afternoon. When we got home, however, Nic was there and had brought us dinner. I suspected that he wanted to talk about the family business.

Lilac went upstairs to her room after dinner, leaving Nic, Bubba, and I sitting in the living room, talking. Dr. Dexter was sitting next to me on the couch but I suspected that Fluffy had followed Lilac upstairs. The cat loved the attention she got from Lilac, and she was probably trying to make Bubba jealous. Cats were like that.

"So do you want me to leave you two alone?" Bubba asked, standing near the doorway, a cup of coffee in his hand.

"I think you need to know what's going on as much as I do." I met Nic's gaze, and he nodded. "So come sit down and hear all about our dysfunctional family."

"All families are dysfunctional if you dig deep enough." Bubba sat on the other end of the couch. Then he blushed. "Don't tell my mom I said that. She thinks we're perfect."

"Our mother thought the same thing." Nic chuckled as he pulled out a notebook. "Okay, so I canceled the board meeting and sent everyone home. However, some of the locals still want to do dinner on Friday night. So please, keep that on your schedule."

I had my planner on the coffee table so I circled the dinner and crossed off the board meeting. "I appreciate you letting me know. The Clayborne Estate is going to be more labor intensive than I thought. So that gives me a full day to work on plans and schedules."

"Am I off full time coverage?" Bubba asked. Dr. Dexter had left my side and was now next to Bubba who was rubbing the dog's back with his free hand.

"Not quite yet." Nic leaned back and looked at the stairwell. "We think Lilac's friend, Skye was working with a street group that was scamming tourists. The girls would set up the mark, tell a fortune with Tarot, then when the tourist pulled out their wallet to pay them, someone run by and relieve them of it and their money. We believe that the group was one of several set up by Uncle Arthur."

"We have legitimate shops that service the tourists to find out their future. Why would someone trust a reading off the street?" I leaned forward and took a drink of my coffee.

"I hear the price is compelling." Nic shrugged. "Why would anyone go to a fortune teller in the first place? It's a fun activity to tell their friends. It's part of our history. And our uncle is making it look like we're all scammers."

I'd met several of the fortune tellers that worked in our shops. Most of them didn't talk to the dead or see ghosts like I did. They watched the reactions of the marks and fed their stories through what most likely was happening. A bride-to-be, visiting with her bachelorette party, was looking for assurance she was about to marry Mr. Right. An older woman was looking for love in her future. A man was looking for confidence that this was the perfect job. People wanted to know they were on the right path. "Mom always said we were there to give people hope, not an accurate vision of their future."

"That's nice." Bubba smiled at me.

"Well, Uncle Arthur would say there's a sucker born every minute.

I need to get home." Nic stood. "I've got feelers out with law enforcement and have made it clear that Ardronic Enterprises isn't associated with or condoning the street group. So if our uncle is behind this, he's on his own. Which is where I want to keep it. Just be careful."

After Nic left, I took Dr. Dexter out to the back yard before heading to bed. As I sat on the deck, watching him, I heard someone on the other side of the barrier that separated the two decks. I stepped off into the grass so I could see the other deck and its occupants. "I hear you over there."

Alexander Morgan stepped off the deck and into the yard, meeting me by the fence. "I didn't mean to scare you."

"Right now or this afternoon at the bridge?"

He chuckled. "I thought you might have seen me. I was following your young friend for over an hour without being seen, but when you show up, you see me in less than ten minutes. I wonder what that says?"

"About you or me?" I grabbed a lawn chair and sat. He mirrored my actions. "Why were you following Lilac?"

"I'm trying to catch a monster."

His honesty surprised me and it must have shown, even in the dim light from the deck because he laughed.

"I guess that wasn't what you were expecting me to say." He leaned closer to the fence between us. Dr. Dexter lifted his head from where he was lying, then settled back down. Apparently, he didn't sense a threat.

"I thought maybe you were the monster." I admitted, letting the words I'd been thinking settle between us. "You *are* a mystery, Mr. Morgan."

"I'm an enigma, a paradox. A man who owns a very nice condo that I'm never living in. I do have a job that takes me all over the world." He was studying me, I could feel his gaze.

"A job for Charming Homes?" I guessed. "Not an interior designer, correct?"

He didn't say anything for a while. "I should have guessed that you'd do some research on me and the company that sold you the house. I suspect you know it's warded by now."

"I knew before I bought it. I thought it strange, but it worked for me, so I just assumed either you or the prior resident needed some protection from the other side. And since all the other residents had just rented the house, odds were it was you who had it warded." I couldn't believe I was telling him all this. Maybe he was compelling me to talk. But with the wards, I knew that wasn't possible. Wards not only protected me from spirits, but it also meant that spells couldn't be cast on the property. Or more accurately, they wouldn't work. "You're easy to talk to."

This time the laugh was full on. "I've never been told that before. No, I'm not a monster and, since we're being honest, yes, I work for Charming Homes. They have a number of services, one, being the warding of houses for a special class of people."

"Like the Clayborne Estate." I said confirming the information I'd gotten off the business card.

He sighed. "I have a feeling they aren't going to like you knowing so much. Especially since your family owns Ardronic Enterprises. It could be seen as a conflict of interest."

"My brother runs the family business. Not me. I'm an interior designer. I found your company's card at the estate today." I felt like being open might give me the information I was looking for as well.

He nodded although I could faintly see the movement in the dim lighting. "I'd heard you were taking on that project. You shouldn't have any ghost issues there, not now."

"Did you ward the property? Is that why you're here?" I watched as he stood and moved his chair back in line with the others.

"No. I don't work in the warding division. That's a different specialty. I told you what I do." He stood and moved the chair back to the grouping that sat around a fire pit in his lawn. "Good night, Miss Cayce."

I watched him leave and wondered if he was being totally truthful. If he was, then I lived next to a man who did a job I'd only heard about from my mother. A fable, a fantasy, a children's story.

Alexander Morgan hunted monsters.

THE NEXT MORNING, I had time for coffee and a chat with Lilac before our trio needed to catch a streetcar to work. I was trying to walk the fine edge between the truth and scaring the girl to death. Whatever would keep her safe.

She dumped the remainder her coffee down the drain. "I get it. No wandering off. No talking to ghosts. Just go to work and come home. So, basically, I'm grounded."

"If you want to go out, just let me know and we'll set up a security detail for you." I had my planner open and was staring at the three back-to-back interviews Mel had set up for me today. It's not that I don't like people, okay, so really, it is that I don't like people. Hiring so far had worked out. But how long would I be lucky in my choices?

"You want someone to follow me and watch me buy groceries?" Lilac rolled her eyes.

"We can have groceries delivered. Besides, it's not forever. Just until Nic can get the target off our backs." I shut my planner and stood, filling a travel mug. "I know you don't like it, but can you do this for me? For a little bit longer?"

She closed her eyes, then stomped off without answering. I heard a muttered, 'Whatever," as she walked toward the living room.

"Great!" I grabbed my planner and stuffed it into my tote. Then I checked the lock on the back door. I hurried after her and found her and Bubba in the living room. "Time to get on our way. Who's ready for an amazing day?"

"Me, me, pick me." Bubba jumped up and down, his right hand in the air.

Lilac burst out laughing at his antics. "You're such a dork."

"I know you are, but what am I?" Bubba shot back at her, making her laugh even more.

"Okay, kids, time to get into work." I followed everyone into the foyer. Dr. Dexter and Fluffy sat on the stairs, watching us. "Sorry, no pets allowed on the streetcar. Besides, mommy's busy trying to hire new friends for you to meet."

Dr. Dexter laid down, his head between his feet and ignored me. Fluffy already was ignoring anyone and anything that might be close to being human. I was certain as soon as the front door shut they'd be having the animal version of a toga party.

"Making friends and influencing people this morning, I see," Bubba whispered to me as we walked out of the house and I paused to lock the door and set the alarm.

"Don't start. It's not my fault Nic wants us under protection for the next few weeks, but he's insistent so I'm going to honor his wishes." I glanced back at Alexander's side of the house and saw a shape in one of the upstairs window, watching us leave. *Monster hunter.* What did that even mean?

"Are you okay?" Bubba had stopped walking and was staring up at the now empty window.

"I'm fine," I said, shaking off the feeling of being watched. "I just need to call Annamae when I get to the office. Can you remind me?"

"Of course." He took my arm and nodded to the nearest cross street. "The streetcar is arriving soon, we should hurry." We walked the rest of the way to the stop in silence. I climbed on the streetcar and greeted our regular driver. Lilac sat on the other side of the trolly car and turned her head away from us. She stayed that way until we got off at our stop, then she walked five steps ahead of us.

"Don't get too far ahead," Bubba called after her and to my surprise, Lilac slowed down her pace. I knew she wanted to find out what happened to her friend. I felt overwhelmed by too many people with too many needs surrounding me. Nic's issues with the family business, Lilac's loss of her friend, my own business. Then there was the conversation with my neighbor.

I smiled and started walking faster. Annamae was the only one I could trust to ask. With my parents and grandparents gone, and my aunts and uncles in an all-out war with us, the only one who had lived through the early years when my parents were setting up the company. And she believed in all kinds of magic, not just my ability to see the dead.

When I was a child, she'd been the one to comfort me when a random ghost would show up and ruin my day. She told me that my gift was special. That I could help the ghosts finish their work and cross over. She was also the only one to warn me about the others. "The world isn't just filled with the living and the dead. You need to protect yourself from the others who want to spread their evil on good people."

The memory of her words made me reach for the amulet that she'd given me so many years ago. A silver pendant that circled a large tree. She'd told me it was my protection, and after I'd brought Lilac home, I noticed that Annamae had given her one as well. Nic didn't have a charm around his neck but he had a matching tattoo on his arm. It was time to find out what it meant and who, I was being protected from.

I pulled out the chain and rubbed the charm between my fingers as we walked the last few blocks to the shop. Monsters, killers, random ghosts, my relatives. Coming back to New Orleans had put me into the middle of a war where I didn't understand the rules. It was time for a deep dive into what was really going on here.

Right after I finished my hiring interviews and finished up inventory with Lilac. Oh, and finished the design plans for the Clayborne house. Real life to dos.

First up, a call to Annamae. I had a feeling that if I put this off, the other side of my life was going to take over my daily to do list.

When I got to the shop and unlocked the door, Mel was already at her desk working. She glanced at her watch as she stood to greet us. "Go ahead and leave the door open. I just got a call from Danny and he's on his way over."

Bubba hesitated but followed Mel's instructions. He looked at me. "Can we all stay on this floor until I have a chance to walk the building?"

"Seriously?" I turned back to challenge him, but the look on his face made me change my mind. Something had spooked him from the time we got onto the streetcar. "Fine, sorry. I get it, you're here to protect us. Lilac? Can I trust you on inventory today or are you going to disappear on us again?"

"I'm not going anywhere. I learned my lesson yesterday. Besides, Kirk said if I pulled a stunt like that again, he'd be disappointed." Lilac eyes widened and I realized all of us were staring at her. She sank into a chair by Mel's desk. "What? I don't want to let him down. He does so much for everyone, it's like disappointing Santa Claus or something."

"Oh, to have my words not fall on deaf ears." I opened my planner and sat next to Lilac. "I'm just kidding. I know it's been a hard week for all of us."

"I can't believe Skye is dead. She taught me how to live on the streets when I first got here. She introduced me to Kirk. She said I was too nice to not have a chance at a real life." Tears filled Lilac's eyes. "She believed me when I told her about the ghosts. She said I could make a lot of money here, without scamming anyone."

"Skye didn't have a gift like yours?" This was the most Lilac had ever talked about her friend. I wanted to give her time. "I thought she was doing fortunes?"

"She worked with a guy." Lilac smiled through her tears. "She said her job was like being a hooker, but she worked with people's minds, not their bodies."

"Do you know the guy's name?" I wondered if this was one of the street rings Uncle Arthur was running.

"She called him Ice, but that's all I know. She told me to stay away from those people. A couple of days later, she introduced me to Kirk. And I ended up here." Lilac wiped her face with the back of her hand. "She saved me."

"I think you had a lot of guardian angels who helped you save yourself." Mel handed her a tissue. "But if you take off again like you did yesterday, I'm going to kick your butt. I was so worried."

Lilac snorted as she used the tissue to dry her eyes. "Like you could."

"Oh, missy, I have friends," Mel teased.

"Like me," Bubba added. The doorbell rang and Danny stepped into the shop. He must have felt the emotions all flying around because he froze just inside the door.

"Everything all right here?" His hand drifted to the inside of his coat where his gun was hidden.

"Stand down, it's just a chat session." Bubba nodded to me. "I'm heading upstairs to check out the rest of the building."

"I'll come with you if you can clear my floor first. I need to make a call, then I'll be ready for my first interview." I turned to Mel. "Call me when they arrive. I'll come down and do the interview in the conference room."

"The applications and my notes are in files on your desk." Mel nodded as her phone rang. "And now it's time to get started."

"I'll come up with you. I finished inventory on five but left my stuff on four so I'll start back up there." Lilac stood and followed Bubba and me.

Harry floated with us to the elevator. "I'll watch her and report if she even looks like she's leaving."

"Thanks," I smiled over at the shop ghost who was now Lilac's babysitter.

Bubba frowned at me. "Do you want me to clear four first?"

"No, clear three. Then go up to four. We have someone to watch Lilac for a few minutes." I held open the elevator door and we walked and floated inside. Then I pushed the button for the third and fourth floor.

"I feel like a six-year-old who can't be trusted to stay home alone." Lilac complained.

Bubba and I just stared at her.

"Okay, fine, I deserve that." Lilac leaned on the elevator wall as the doors opened for three. "Harry and I will be on four if you need us."

Bubba watched the elevator close and then turned to me. "Sometimes working with you and the gang is a little unnerving."

I poked him in the side. "I thought you liked Harry."

6

Annamae promised to tell me everything, if I'd come to dinner that night. I explained that I'd have to bring Bubba and Lilac.

"Of course, I was expecting you to say that. Bring that cute dog of yours too. I made some pumpkin treats for him on Saturday." Annamae paused as a bell went off in her kitchen. "I've got to go. I'm baking a cake for dessert tonight."

When I hung up, I opened the first file. The person might be good for the shop, but they didn't have much design experience. I needed someone who had both that could be a floater between the two parts of my business. Or I could train Jennifer in the design side. I sat the folder down and went through the other two.

The last folder intrigued me. The guy had started design school, left before graduation, and had worked at auction houses since. Depending on what he wanted to do, he might fit into both worlds. I noticed that Mel had drawn a star at the top of his application, her signal that she thought he was the best choice.

The good thing about starting a new business was if I liked all three candidates, I had the work to keep all of them busy. The bad thing was I didn't just want to hire warm bodies. So to speak. I wanted people who wanted to build a career with us.

As I was waiting for the first interview to start, I printed off the list of items we had stored on the third floor. The floor only had a small storage area compared to the other three floors, but I could probably complete inventory on this level before the end of the day.

We'd spent hours setting up the inventory program when I'd bought the shop months ago. Okay, Mel had set up the program, and I'd dug through the mass of items the prior owner had horded over the years. It didn't help that his 'trusted' employees had been taking the best items off Matty's hands and selling them off under the table.

This was the third quarterly inventory, and we were still finding items that hadn't been included in our first listing. Maybe fourth time would be the charm. I opened the storage door and turned on the lights. Time to get busy.

When my interview arrived, I stopped at my office first. Washing my hands, I saw a cobweb in my hair. I shook it out, then checked my reflection. Satisfied that I didn't look like I'd been rolling in the dirt, I grabbed the file, a notebook and pen, and a jacket to cover up the shirt that had been whiter when I left home.

Mel was waiting for me at the elevator with the first candidate.

"Joseph Addison, this is Eddie Cayce. She's the owner and will be doing your interview today." Mel introduced us as I stepped off the elevator.

He held out his hand. "Eddie Cayce? Like Edward Cayce? Are you related?"

I smiled and nodded. "Distantly. Let's go into the conference room and talk. Do you want coffee or water?"

"Water will be great. I did a paper on Edward Cayce. I didn't know he had roots in New Orleans." Joseph chatted on about his studies as we made our way to the conference room.

I grabbed two bottles of water from the mini fridge and handed him one. "Let's talk about the job. What brought you to apply?"

The water lasted longer than the interview. Joseph was not a good match for the team. I thanked him for coming in and told him I'd have an answer by next week. He grinned and strolled out of the shop, pulling his phone out as soon as he was in the main sales floor. "Dude, you won't believe who I just talked to."

I paused at Mel's desk and gave her back the file. After Joseph had left the building, I signed. "Send him a no thank you letter next week."

"Not a good fit?"

I sat down, closing my eyes and leaning my head back. "Not even close."

"Hiring good employees makes the rest of your job easier." Harry said.

I opened my eyes and saw him hovering above me. "Thanks for the advice. Aren't you supposed to be watching Lilac?"

"She's coming down the elevator now. I'm just faster." Harry grinned then disappeared.

Mel was watching me. "I take it Harry's nearby?"

Shrugging I stood up to watch the elevator descend. "He was. He took off. Lilac's on her way down. Where's Bubba?"

"He left to pick up our lunch order. Danny's over by the door if you need something." Mel pointed out the tall, well-built man watching us talk. "He's kind of cute, isn't he?"

"Does somebody have a crush?" I turned to watch Mel blush.

"Do you know how hard it is to meet someone at my age? I can't talk to guys at a bar because I don't know if they're just tourists. I didn't go to school here. I'm not into league sports." She leaned back into her chair. "Could you ask Bubba if Danny's married or seeing someone?"

"Definitely. Better you find that out now than waste any more of that perfume. What is it you're wearing?" I leaned closer, trying to identify the smell.

"Expensive. That's all you need to know. Besides, they call all these perfumes stupid names like Desire or Need." She shook her head as I started to laugh. "Okay, it's Desire. Stop talking about my perfume."

"I'm going upstairs to finish the third-floor inventory list and taking Lilac with me. That way, you two can be alone." I stood and checked my watch. "My next interview should be here at eleven. I'll eat after that. Call me when she's here."

The second interview no showed. So Lilac and I had lunch with the group before my third appointment was scheduled. The call came ten minutes early. I glanced over at Lilac who was looking up a midcentury nightstand. "Will you be okay here by yourself?"

"You don't have to send Harry to watch me. He keeps telling me stories about the way women dressed in his day. You would think I was running around naked."

"You are showing a lot of leg," Harry appeared next to me.

"And you're eavesdropping." Lilac pointed out.

"Harry, shorts are appropriate for women now." I pointed to Lilac's tank and short set. "And she does a lot of furniture moving and not a lot of sales."

"My wife moved furniture and cleaned the shop in full skirts and a corset." Harry sniffed.

"Still, stop giving Lilac trouble about her clothes." I handed Lilac my checklist. "You can stay and help her identify pieces if you want."

"Thanks," Lilac muttered.

I smiled sweetly. "Oh, and we're going to the compound for dinner tonight. Annamae insists."

"That's the best news I've heard today." Lilac brightened as she took my list and combined it with hers. "I'll be downstairs as soon as I'm finished."

"The way the interviews are going, I might be back before you're done." I headed to the hallway and to my office to clean up again before the interview.

Harry followed me. "You need to go into each interview with high hopes. You may miss a gem if you keep expecting to be disappointed. Back in the day..."

Harry kept talking all the way to the elevator and only stopped when Mel walked up to greet me with a familiar face in tow. I glanced at the job application, realizing I'd skipped the name and just reviewed his background. "Will Marshall? Is that you? I didn't know you were in town?"

He gave me a hug. "I'm so glad you remember me. It's been a while."

I turned to Mel who was watching us with amusement. "Will was in my Design 101 class freshman year. We did our first project together."

"I was the organizer of a bunch of cats. But we got it done, even though out of the group of five, it was mostly the two of us who did the work." Will grinned at the memory. "I don't think any of our group beside Eddie graduated with a design degree."

"The others weren't really interested in the work. What happened to you? I came back for Sophomore year, and you weren't there." I nodded toward the conference room. "Hold that thought, we'll get started on the interview and get caught up at the same time. Water? Coffee?"

He accepted the water and sat down at the table. "I ran out of money. I had access to my entire college fund day one and spent the whole amount in one year. After that, I came home and started working at the auction house. I'm back in school at nights to get the degree."

"I'm glad. You are really talented. Tell me what you want to do for a career? What's the dream?" I hadn't realized Will was from New Orleans. Or maybe I'd forgotten. That might have been what brought us together in that class.

We sat and talked for over an hour, then I took Will on a tour of the shop and to meet the rest of the crew. Harry was hanging around in my office as we finally sat again. I pulled out a hiring package and handed Will the paperwork. "If you want the job, it's yours. I can keep you busy forty plus hours a week. Can you start next week?"

"I need to give two weeks' notice." Will glanced at his phone. "But I can give notice today if that works?"

I agreed and gave him the salary and benefits package discussion. Nic let me use Ardronic's benefit program so at least I could offer my staff a good package. After I explained that, I pulled out another form. "Sign this and I'll reimburse you for tuition and books."

"For a small company, you have a lot of benefits." Will beamed as he signed all the forms.

"I want to keep my employees happy." I took all the paperwork and put it back in the folder so I could give it to Mel. "Oh, and better news, we'll be working on the Clayborne Estate when you start so I'll probably put you on that with me first project."

His eyes widened. "That would be amazing. I've always wanted to see the inside of that place. Isn't it haunted?"

"I've heard that, but doesn't every old house have a story?" Even though Will was a friend, he didn't know about my gifts. That was a conversation I kept pretty close, especially in Seattle where I was trying to avoid that side of my personality.

He stood and followed me to the front. "I've heard a lot of stories since I moved here. Thanks for taking a chance on me. I promise, you won't regret it."

Will walked out of the shop and he pulled out his phone, calling someone to tell them the good news. As I watched, I wondered if it was his girlfriend, or mother, or – my breath caught. Could he have been sent by Uncle Arthur or maybe Aunt Franny? Will didn't look back as he took the call but something in my gut was warning me.

Mel came to join me where I was standing, frozen. I'd been in such a good mood when I'd hired him. It could be just a bad feeling, but I'd learned to trust those feelings after leaving Seattle. I handed her the folder. "Hey, do me a favor and have Nic's team do a full back-ground check on Will? I'd like to have the results before he starts week after next Wednesday."

"Something bothering you?" Mel watched as Will got into a car that had pulled over to pick him up.

"Yes." I admitted as I turned toward her. "I'll be upstairs in my office if you need anything."

I could feel Mel's gaze on my back as I walked toward the elevator. I couldn't tell her what was wrong, because I didn't know. Maybe it was nothing. But it was odd for a friend from Seattle to show up here in New Orleans looking for a job.

As soon as we got home, a knock on my front door announced Alexander Morgan's arrival. We were picking up Dr. Dexter and checking on Fluffy before heading over to the family compound for dinner.

"Alexander, I'm sorry, I'm on my way out again." I leaned against the doorway watching the man who'd just confessed to be a monster killer. I wondered what monster he was tracking here in New Orleans.

"I'm just dropping off the file I got from the directors. Lilac's friend isn't the first person to be killed this way in the last three months. I think you should call your police friend and see if they've put together the deaths yet." He handed out a folder toward me.

"This is unexpected. I'm an interior designer, not an investigator." I considered not taking the folder, but then took it anyway. Who was I kidding. Whatever was going on, it was better to have more information than less. Even if I wasn't involved in the investigation. I stepped out onto the porch, hoping Lilac wasn't listening.

"You really don't see yourself that way, do you?" He chuckled. "I guess you're still in the deny stage of finding your true purpose."

"That's a little presumptuous, isn't it?" Anger tinted my words, but he'd started it. "I know who I am. And my role here isn't as the supernatural police for the area. Although it seems like you hold that badge."

"It's not a badge, and to be perfectly honest, my responsibilities don't just cover New Orleans. I'll put it in terms you'll hate. You're local enforcement, I'm international." He turned and stepped off my deck and crossed the grass to his own steps. When he reached them, he turned toward me and met my gaze. "All I'm asking for is for you read the file and pass the information on to Detective Charles. Your future is still in your own hands."

I watched him go inside, then opened the file. The pictures were horrific. I quickly closed it again and went inside the living room. I tucked it into my tote and realized that Bubba was watching me.

"What's that?" He nodded to the tote where I'd put the file.

I could lie, but he'd see right through it. "Alexander dropped off some information he wants me to look at."

"He's an issue." Bubba went to the front window and scanned the yard. "What's in the folder?"

"Horrible images. If you want to look through it with me after we get back, I'd appreciate it. For now, where's Lilac? Annamae doesn't like us to be late for dinner." I grabbed a jacket and put a leash on Dr. Dexter who was sitting at my feet, whining. He knew we were going somewhere and since I'd picked up the leash, he knew he was going as well.

We got into Bubba's SUV, or the one the company assigned him, and headed toward the family compound. I texted Nic to let him know our ETA and he responded back with 'we need to talk.'

"Of course, we do, that's why I'm coming to dinner," I muttered as I tucked the phone back into my tote.

"Nic?" Bubba chuckled.

"Isn't it always. If I'm upset about something, Captain Obvious knows. I need to be better at a consistent block of my thoughts." I closed my eyes and imagined a brick wall.

"Like that's going to do any good." Tessa Hunt said from behind me.

I heard Lilac squeak as she turned to see the ghost sitting next to her. Dr. Dexter was by the window, so Tessa had to materialize between them. "Tessa, what are you doing here? I thought maybe you'd crossed over since I hadn't seen you for a while."

"You live in a warded house. How am I supposed to just drop in?" Tessa leaned over and looked at Bubba who was ignoring the conversation since he knew I was chatting up a ghost he couldn't hear or see. "He's a hottie. And he's not a cop. You really should seal that deal before he finds someone he likes better."

Lilac started laughing and I felt my face turn red.

"I take it my presence has been noticed?" Bubba said as he turned the car onto the freeway.

"Shut up." I turned to face Tessa. "So are you just here to torment me or do you have something to tell me?"

"Wow. A girl just teases you about the hottie hanging around all the time and this is what I get? Attitude?" Tessa grinned and shot a look at Lilac. "Your friend is gone. I don't know who has been impersonating her, but I talked to someone who saw her leave. There's a group of souls that maintain that section of the French Quarter. They help those that are lost, leave. They've approached me several times, but I'm not ready."

"Wait. That's a lot of information. Souls hang around to ease the transition?" Grandma Andrews had never told me this. But maybe she hadn't known.

"Skye's really gone then?" Lilac sank back into her seat. "I was hoping, I mean, I don't want her to stay around just for me. But I hoped I could talk to her at least once."

Tessa patted at Lilac's hand. "The good thing is she didn't suffer. The death was violent and according to the Knights, people who die like that are better off going early. Or bad things can happen."

"The Knights? That's what they call themselves?" I knew Lilac was mourning the loss of her friend, again, but I was focused on what Tessa knew about this group.

Tessa nodded and started to fade out. "You're driving out of my area. I'll try to visit the shop tomorrow if the wards haven't been reset."

"Knights, huh? That's new." Bubba said as Tessa slowly disappeared.

I nodded, thinking about what she'd said. Then I realized the main point I'd missed. "Wait, Tessa, are wards set on the shop?"

7

L ilac looked a little less upset when we got to the compound. I found Nic as soon as we arrived and cornered him in his office, alone. "Why didn't you tell me you put wards on the shop?"

He closed out the computer file he'd been working on before we arrived and then stood, coming around his desk to give me a hug. "Nice to see you too, sis. Sorry, I don't know about any wards on your shop. You told me you didn't want that level of protection because it might affect Harry's ability to wander or cross over."

"I know I said that, so why did you put wards up?"

"You're not listening." He nodded to a leather wing back chair by the fireplace in his office. My brother was all about appearances. Even at home. "Sit down. I have a feeling this is going to be a long conversation."

He sat in a matching chair and waited for me to sit as well. I took off my jacket since he'd had a fire lit in the fireplace and the room was toasty. "Okay, now why do you think you have wards on the shop? And why do you think it was me?"

"Tessa told me that she can't come into the shop because of the wards. Or exactly, she said she'd see me tomorrow if my wards on the shop were down. I don't have wards on the shop." I carefully folded my jacket across my lap. "And I can't have wards because there was a spirit besides Harry there talking to Lilac yesterday. She thought it was Skye but according to Tessa, Skye crossed over. She said the Knights told her."

"Okay, I can't verify the Skye thing, but the Knights are real. Tessa said she talked to them? That's strange. I've never heard a firsthand account of the Knights talking to a soul. However, most of the souls they approach take their advice and move on." Nic rubbed a spot on his armrest. "Why is Tessa staying? Are we sure it's Tessa? You said the other ghost wasn't Skye."

"I don't know that answer, but from my interaction with her just now, I believe it's really her. She's just so Tessa." I grinned at the memory of her teasing me about Bubba.

"I'll stop by tomorrow and see if I can feel out the wards. If they're from our corporation, they'll have a signature. They could be by the Charming Homes Corporation." He leaned forward. "That's what I wanted to talk to you about. Your neighbor and his assertion that he's a monster hunter."

"I really have to learn to build a better wall to keep you out of my thoughts." I leaned forward, watching the fire and matching Nic's stance. "Anyway, what do you know?"

"Mom told me stories about a group who fought monsters. I figured it was a fairy tale. You got the princesses locked up in towers that saved themselves and I got stories about knights and monster hunters that saved the world." He stood and pulled out a couple of books. "I thought they were just stories, then I found these. They're narratives about monsters and how they were killed. It's got a list of hunters that gave their lives in the back of this book. And there's an Alexander Morgan the second, listed a few hundred years ago."

"You think my neighbor either took his name as a cover, or is from the linage?" I opened one of the books and paged through the items. It was written in the form of a journal, or a diary of wars and monsters killed. If I replaced the words, vampires or weres, with

Indians or British, I could be looking at a revolutionary war diary of a general. "This looks real."

"It is real. There's a lot we need to talk about," Annamae stood at the open door. "But dinner's on the table and it's time to eat. No used going into this on an empty stomach."

Nic and I followed her toward the dining room. I'd put the books into my tote and put that with my jacket on a chair in the living room. I guess it was time to find out the rest of my family heritage since it wasn't going to just go away. No matter how much I wished it.

Tonight, Annamae sat with us at dinner. She usually ate in the kitchen alone or ate at home. But tonight, she was taking her place as part of the family. A step that should have happened years ago. She focused the conversation on light topics, with the exception of asking Lilac to tell her about her friend, Skye.

Through tears, Lilac painted us a picture of the girl who'd helped Lilac settle into the homeless world of New Orleans and how she'd connected her with Kirk who'd ultimately brought her to me and my shop.

Annamae patted my hand. "You have your mother's gift of bringing people to you. People who need you and who you need. Lilac, you're a part of this family now, as well as Bubba and even you, Dr. Dexter. The strength of family isn't in the blood you're born with, instead it's in the connections you make. One decision at a time. Now, you can leave your family behind, but it's always there, helping you. Being part of your story."

"That's beautiful," Lilac said, drying her eyes. "My grandmother used to say something similar. That I'd find my people when I needed them. I thought it meant my mom would wake up and see me, but instead, I wound up here and found all of you."

Bubba nudged her with his shoulder. "You're all right, kid."

"You're a pain," Lilac responded. "And you're at the table too, so I wouldn't be all that."

"I am all that." Bubba grinned, but then he nodded. "I know I'm paid for my work for security by Mr. Andronic and the company, but that doesn't matter. I am committed to making sure you're all safe. No matter what. Besides, you gave my mom a job and she was driving me crazy by remodeling my apartment every year. I appreciate that more than you know."

"Heather's a valuable asset to our work family." I shook my head. "No, it's not a work family. It's just family. That's why it's been so hard for me to hire someone else. I trust everyone I hired so far with my life. And mostly, with my secrets."

"Well, this got a little touchy feely for me," Nic stood and took my plate along with his own. "Shall we move on to desserts and the subject of the night, monster killers?"

The group stood over Annamae's objections and took their empty plates into the kitchen where they were rinsed and put into the dishwasher. I showed Lilac where the desserts plates were kept and we grabbed the apple pie as well as vanilla ice cream and whipped cream to take out to the dining room.

Bubba grabbed cups and Annamae filled a carafe with coffee and set up cream and sugar bowls. We were all back in our places with dessert in front of us in less than ten minutes. I nodded to Annamae. "So my neighbor says he and Charming Homes protect the world from monsters. What do you know about that?"

Annamae sipped her coffee. "Your parents were called monsters when they started the fortune telling business here in New Orleans. People thought they were using those with talents to scam people who believed. But your dad always wanted it to be legitimate. He wanted to help others. Your uncle? He just saw the money in the business. Your Aunt Franny, well, you know that your grandmother basically disowned your aunt when she used her talents to scam that rich guy into marrying her. Ms. Andrews was fit to be tied when she came home with that rock."

"And that's why I have the power and not my aunt." I held up my coffee cup. "Lucky me."

"You never used your powers to your own benefit. Even as a kid, we'd hear you trying to talk souls to go into the light. That they'd be happier there." Annamae smiled at me. "You are a kind soul. That's why your grandmother wanted you to have the power."

"And that's why we can't let Uncle Arthur take over the business. It's a fight between doing good and making money. We have enough money. We pay our employees well. We don't need more. But he's all about his dividend check." Nic pushed a piece of apple around his plate. "I want to raise kids who are proud of their family heritage. Not conflicted."

"Are you telling us a secret?" I grinned at Annamae.

"No. I mean, you know Esmeralda. She's stubborn." He shook his head. "Tonight's getting off the rails. So our folks wanted the best out of us. We get that. What about the monsters?"

"Your mom and dad knew about Charming Homes. And the Knights." Annamae nodded at me. "They would have told you everything, but then, they were taken before their time. And you were left with the fairy tales. There is a long history of human knights who save the world from the beasts who decided they want to live in the dark. And then, when the human lives end, they become knights on the other side. They help transition the lost souls. I believe your neighbor may be one of these knights."

"Knights in New Orleans?" I clarified.

Annamae shook her head. "Oh, no dear. The knights are everywhere."

THERE WAS MUCH MORE to say, but we were all tired and our brains hurt from the new information. I still had the file from Alexander to look at and decide if I was going to pass on to Boone. And if I was, how it was going to happen. And now, I had homework to read and absorb before I ran into my neighbor again.

I was convinced he was on the side of good. But even I wasn't so naïve to not understand that sometimes, being on the side of good meant doing things that in ordinary cases would be considered bad. Like taking a life if they had turned into a monster.

And what made someone irredeemable? Was it one sin? Was it many? Was it in the nature of non-humans? And if so, what did that mean in my own life? Did the power I possessed put me on the path to be a monster? Or was I already deemed that, no matter what actions I took or performed with the supernatural power?

It was all giving me a headache. Or it could have been the sugar rush from the ice cream and apple pie. Either way, I decided to close my eyes on the way home and let the ideas float around rather than figuring out what I needed to do tomorrow.

Tonight, I'd sleep on it. Tomorrow, I'd go to work and finish up the planning for the Clayborne Estate. Then I'd get dressed up and have dinner with a group of board members that I didn't know if they were on our side or not.

Yeah, life was getting interesting.

The next morning, breakfast in the kitchen was quiet. All of us had a lot of processing to do. Instead of joining them, I headed to my home office with a cup of coffee and thumbed through the file. There had been several bodies found in New Orleans in the last few months. All of the women had been killed the same way Skye had and left by the river for someone to find. The police were looking for a building where the murders were actually committed since they thought the river was a body dump. I scanned through the pictures. Young women, not much more than kids, really. All were pretty before this killer got to them. And, as I read the backgrounds of the victims, all had been working as a street fortune teller.

"Are you about ready? We have thirty minutes until the next streetcar." Bubba leaned against the doorway to my office, drinking his coffee. "You should eat something."

"I'm not hungry." I pushed the folder toward him. "Read the first three summaries and tell me what the young women have in common. Besides being attractive, young, and dead."

He frowned but came into my office and set his coffee on my desk. Then he started reading. As he did, I tucked the Clayborne file into my tote. I was hoping to get back out to the estate now that we'd been given the green light by Eliza through email. The only thing on today's schedule right now was the new client walk through at a remodel project in the French Quarter a few blocks from my shop. I'd dressed in a linen suit, hoping to project a professional image, but I think with the humidity mixed with today's heat, I might just look like a drowned rat by the ten o'clock meeting.

I scanned my email on my phone as I waited for Bubba to finish reading. He turned the fourth page, scanned and then set the folder on the desk. "All of them were working as street fortune tellers?"

"What do you want to bet they are part of my uncle's under the table group that Nic's been so upset about?" I stood and slid the folder over to me where I tucked it into my bag as well. "I should have had Nic look at this last night. I don't know what he can do about Uncle Arthur, but there has to be something."

"It doesn't make sense." Bubba said as we moved to the kitchen to collect Lilac and lock up the house.

"Why's that?" I put a yogurt into a baggie and held it up to Bubba before I put it into my tote, I didn't want any complaining about me not eating.

"These girls were making someone money. The only person who would want them dead is the competition. Which in this case, isn't your uncle, it's your brother."

I turned and stared at him. "There's no way Nic would be involved in anything like this."

"Maybe not, but my logic still holds. Why would you kill someone who was making you money? You wouldn't unless you didn't care about money. From what I've seen, that doesn't describe your uncle." Bubba locked the front door and handed me back my keys. Lilac was already almost at the sidewalk.

A cloud emerged on the sidewalk and hovered in place like it was waiting for her. I frowned, trying to listen to the multitudes of voices that were screaming at me. "Lilac, don't step past the hedge."

It looked like she was disorientated due to the large number of voices and my words, while they slowed her, they didn't stop her. Bubba started toward her but all of a sudden someone ran past us and pulled her out of the cloud that had started to engulf her. We gathered around her in the yard. Lilac took a big breath and then another. Finally, she looked up at me.

"That was intense. I could hear all the voices. So many voices. They were crying for help. They wanted me to save them." Lilac said as she leaned against Alexander who had been the one to pull her out. "What's going on?"

Alexander let go of her arms and stepped back, giving Lilac time to stand on her own. "I believe they were here to collect you. You have been digging up information on the murders. This group, well, it's under the spell of those who killed them. The one that killed your friend. I believe, they are acting under a compulsion from their master."

"The killer?" The file in my tote felt heavy. Maybe I should have let Lilac in on the murders. Told her to be careful. Locked her in the warded house. "Why are they targeting Lilac?"

Alexander watched the cloud disappear from the front of the house. He didn't answer until they were all gone. "Lilac must know something the killer doesn't want her to tell anyone."

Lilac shook her head. "I don't know anything."

"I think we need to talk about your friend. Can I accompany you all to the streetcar?" Alexander held out his arm for Lilac.

I turned to Bubba. "Do you think it's safe?"

He shrugged. "You'll have to ask Mr. Morgan. The woo woo part is someone else's job. I'm here to keep you safe from normal things, like sniper rifles or speeding cars."

"I assure you both that it's perfectly safe now. The ghosts need to recharge before they could stage a second attack. And, since we're aware of their existence, even that's going to be hard for them." Alexander scanned the street before stepping off the warded part of the property. "I have to admit, we thought you would be a quiet neighbor when we allowed you to purchase the condo. Having someone who understands what Mr. King calls the woo woo part is usually an advantage. I didn't expect this string of murders in the quarter to be so closely tied to you, Miss Cayce."

"It's not her fault," Lilac smiled at me as we walked toward the corner. "It's mine. I befriended Skye. And I let Eddie talk me into moving in with her. I bet you regret that now."

"I do not. Lilac, you're family now. Good or bad, you're part of our crew. So get used to it." Lilac flashed me a grateful smile and Bubba patted my shoulder. Apparently, I'd said the right thing.

I glanced around the neighborhood and saw the ghost that had told me about Alexander being here standing and watching us from the other side of the street. Had she been part of the crowd?

The streetcar was almost at our stop so we dropped the conversation and hurried to board it. We were the only ones on as the car turned around and headed back into town. As we stopped to pick up other riders, I thought about what might have happened to Lilac and the thoughts made me shiver.

Lilac must have sensed my emotion as she looked up from showing Alexander her design book and met my gaze. I returned it with as much happiness and joy as I could force into an emotion. A bunch of terrorists ghosts were not going to derail our day. Not today.

8

Lilac and I were working on a new hire training checklist for Will's start in two weeks. She wasn't supposed to work today, but with everything that had been going on, I wasn't going to leave her at the house. Even though she'd be protected as long as she didn't leave. It was that slim chance that she'd decide to run to the store to grab something for dinner or get a call from a friend that worried me. I know, mother henning, but then again, we had been attacked by a swarm of ghosts this morning. I bet that challenge wasn't in the parenting books on how to deal with a teenager.

When Harry showed up floating above my desk, I remembered what Tessa had said about the shop. Someone had warded it. "Hey Harry, have you tried leaving lately?"

"Now why would I want to do that. The outside world is so chaotic now adays. Cars and people line the streets like it's Mardi Gras every night. I'd rather stay here and read. That was a nice collection of books you bought from that estate sale last month." Harry looked over Lilac's shoulder. "I can't believe those computer things actually caught on. Now you're doing everything on that picture screen. What happened to good old pen and paper?"

"Oh, I still use it to send letters and brainstorm," Lilac set the laptop on my desk and stretched. "I'm going down to get a water. Do you want anything?"

"I'm good." I picked up my coffee travel mug that was still half full from when I'd filled it this morning at the shop.

"You should drink more water," Lilac said as she left the office. "Oh, and goodbye, Harry. Unless you're still going to be here when I get back."

"We'll see. I have a few things to discuss with Miss Cayce here." Harry smiled as Lilac left the office and headed to the stairs. "It's nice to have young people around that can actually hear me. She's a treasure, that one. And so polite."

"She is pretty special." I turned back to the subject at hand. "So you didn't notice any wards blocking ghosts from coming in? Or when they might have been set?"

Harry focused on the exterior wall that ran the length of my office. He held his hand up, feeling the energy. "Now that you mention it, there are wards here. I suspect since you're asking me about them that you didn't set them."

"No, and I'm not sure who or why they're here." I glanced at my calendar. "The ghost that pretended to be Skye and led Lilac away, she's not still here, is she?"

"Oh, that would be bad." He disappeared for a few minutes, then returned. "No, I'm the only non-corporal entity in the building. That horrid woman, Tessa, she's outside on the sidewalk. I can see her pacing."

I stifled a chuckle. Tessa was probably bored. I wasn't sure why she hadn't crossed over yet, but I guess that wasn't my decision. "So on Tuesday, a ghost was here talking to Lilac, now, there's a ward on the building to keep them out. That was fast."

"You mean Skye, Lilac's friend?" Harry hovered over a wing back chair next to where Lilac had been sitting.

"I don't think that was Skye." I took out my phone and called Alexander Morgan. He picked up on the third ring.

"I didn't expect to hear from you. Is everything all right?" His voice sounded tight.

I was guessing, but I thought I was right. "I don't know, maybe you can tell me who put a protective ward on my building."

The sigh told me I'd been right.

"It wasn't meant to be intrusive. After that ghost pretended to be Lilac's friend, I thought it would be better to keep any ghost with ulterior motives out of the shop. For your safety, of course."

"Look, I appreciate the concern, but can you please ask me for permission before you go sticking your nose into my business. Or trying to protect me. I've got enough men around who think they know what's best for me." I hung up the phone, not waiting for a response.

Bubba walked into the office. "Okay, I get that you're mad, but I'm just doing my job."

"I'm not mad at you. But one mystery has been solved. Alexander put the wards on the shop to protect us. I guess after seeing what they did this morning, it was probably a good thing to do. I'll apologize tonight when I get home. I might actually mean it by then." I checked my watch. "I take it you're here to remind me about the client meeting?"

"If we're walking, we need to leave soon. Danny is already here and set up downstairs. Mel's getting him coffee. He's not married by the way." He rolled his shoulders. "And Mom's here."

"Sorry, I was supposed to find out and tell her, but I've been a little busy. We better get downstairs then. Or Heather will be making up stories about us." I checked my tote for my notebook and found the file that Alexander had given me earlier that week. I tucked the file into my desk and locked it. "I don't want to accidentally pull that out and scare a client away. I'll be glad when they find whoever killed Skye and we can go back to normal around here."

Bubba mumbled something, but I'd had my back turned and hadn't heard him. I met him at the doorway. "Sorry, what did you say?"

He hurried us to the elevator and pushed the down button. Then he turned toward me. "I said, things are never normal around here. Somedays are just a little quieter than others."

I thought about what he said all the way down to the sales floor. Heather was chatting with Mel as the doors opened and she turned toward the sound, her face flush with anticipation. "Good morning, Heather. Mel, would you please remind Danny that watching Lilac is an important part of his assignment. She is not to leave the building."

Heather grinned at me. "What, did you ground her?"

"Long story. Let's get going."

Heather dug for her keys. "My car's right in front."

"We're walking. And I need a minute, can you and Bubba stay here?" I opened the door and moved over to the flower planter where Tessa was hovering. "What do you need?"

"Well, aren't you direct? I came here to see if you'd let down the wards yet." Tessa folded her arms and hovered above the planter.

"Not yet. I found out who put the wards up and they weren't placed to keep you out. But I'm asking them to keep them up until we've found Skye's killer." I pulled a weed from the planter and took an empty plastic cup out of the vines and put it into the trash.

"What am I supposed to do all day? I can't talk to you during the day because you're working. The house is warded too." Tessa pouted as she hovered.

"Maybe you should think about crossing over." I hoped my voice sounded gentle.

"I'll go hang out at the food court down the street. I love the smells." And with that, Tessa disappeared ignoring my advice.

"Apparently you don't want to talk about the elephant in the room." I called after Tessa and waved at Heather who was watching me out the window. She blushed and nodded. Soon, she and Bubba were standing next to me.

"I wasn't watching you." Heather explained.

I waved away the apology. "Talk to me. You took this call for the new project? What are they looking for?"

Heather nodded and opened a small notebook as we walked. Bubba didn't say anything as he followed along but I imagined he might be calling his mother tonight to talk today's events. Explaining away why I might need some alone time to chat with ghosts without telling her my secrets.

"The woman who called said they wanted to remodel the project for a short-term stay. She said the corporation has employees and clients who come in for meetings and need a place to stay that's more discreet than a hotel." Heather closed the notebook. "So upscale, and classy but other than that, there's no directions. Oh, and she wanted a New Orleans feel to the décor."

"So upscale, but Mardi Gras beads?" Bubba asked from behind us.

I laughed at his comment. "Mardi Gras might be the most famous week of the year here, but there's more to the town than just one continuous party. I'm thinking we'll do modern French. Maybe some antiques, but more comfortable and a place to relax. Don't we still have that Louis the sixteenth replica dining room with the chandelier set up in the shop?"

Heather held up her phone. "I've got several pictures of it here on my phone. So maybe dark blue in the bedroom with a tufted headboard?"

"And we need an office with all the bells and whistles for a busy executive. And a totally modern but French chalet feel kitchen." I could see the final setup in my head. Now I just needed a budget and to take measurements in the house. Hopefully we wouldn't have to do much demolition. Some of the places in the quarter had gotten hit hard in the last hurricane. If this had mold in the walls, the remodel costs just doubled. At least.

Heather pointed to a brick building down the street. "I think that's the address."

Evaluating the outside, I was pleased. It looked like the house had already had a recent remodel. So maybe most of our work would be in changing it from what it had been used for, maybe a private resi-dence, into a more upscale short-term space. A woman stood outside, waiting for us. As we walked up to greet her, a man stepped out of the house, a phone held to his ear. As he turned, I recognized him. Uncle Arthur.

I stopped short and Bubba stepped in front of me. Heather noticed my hesitation and turned back.

"What's wrong?" She looked from me to Uncle Arthur. "Do you know him?"

"That's my uncle." I met Bubba's gaze and realized he was already on high alert and ready to pull me out of the situation. Now I bet he wished we'd driven here because I knew if we had, I would already be in the car, speeding away. I turned to him, trying to get him to calm down. "Let's see what this is about."

I stepped in front of Heather and strolled the rest of the way to where the woman and my uncle stood, waiting for us. When we got there, I smiled at them. "Well, this is a surprise. I didn't know the remodel was for Ardronic Enterprises."

"Good morning, Eddie. The job isn't for Ardronic. It's for my side business. I've been doing some import/export contracts and need a place for my clients to stay when they come into town." Uncle Arthur pulled me into a hug, whispering in my ear. "I hope we can keep this discreet. Your brother and I don't see eye to eye on my endeavors."

I pulled back from the hug, "Can we talk for a minute, alone?"

"Of course, come on in," Uncle Arthur held opened the door and motioned for me to follow him.

I turned to Bubba. "Give me five minutes."

"Eddie," he warned. "I don't think this is a good idea."

"Please?" I waited for his nod and headed inside. "You have five minutes to explain why I wouldn't tell Nic. I don't tell him everything about my business, but I've also never not said something. So what's going on?"

"You have to know we have different visions for the family business."

"Yes. And yet, me renovating a house for you, doesn't seem like a big deal that we need to keep quiet." I wasn't going to just give in. If I was going to hold something back, I needed to know why. And, my uncle needed to know that Nic had access to my thoughts. I had a block on right now that I'd put up as soon as I'd seen Uncle Arthur, but even having that block on was a red flag to Nic.

"Okay, it's not for the business. It's for Tamera." He took a breath. "The woman from Jamaica. I'm setting her up a space here. I'm tired of flying so much. I'd rather your brother not know as it makes me vulnerable."

"I'll keep her out of my thoughts, but he will know I'm working for you. And yes, it's going to be a problem for him as he doesn't trust you right now. And maybe for good reason." I studied my uncle. He knew that I'd known about his girlfriend for years. But I'd never said anything to anyone about what I'd seen. It hadn't been my place to tell. Nic could smell a lie on anyone. It was one of his gifts, to know when someone was truthful. "Maybe if you told him the truth, he wouldn't think of you as untrustworthy."

Uncle Arthur's eyes flashed with anger. Or maybe frustration. But finally, he nodded. "I understand your point. So will you remodel this house for your uncle? I only ask that you don't mention Tamera's involvement. I'll break that to the family in my own way."

"I'd love to remodel this house. Let me get my staff and we'll talk about what your vision is." I dropped my walls and went out to get Bubba and Heather. "Come on in guys, this place is amazing."

We walked through the house and Uncle Arthur told me his vision. I added in what I could and by the end of the tour, I knew I could make this house meet his dream. Now, I just needed to talk money. We gathered at the foyer. "Heather will make up a budget based on what we talked about. Once you approve that, if we find anything additional, like structure issues, we'll come to you with an adjusted budget for your approval before continuing. And we'll give you an estimation of the deadline. After you approve the budget, we'll sign a contract and get this started."

"I don't think we need a formal contract," Uncle Arthur started, but I held up my hand.

"Sorry, I do contracts on everything. That way we both know what we're doing." I shook his hand. "You'll hear from us in a couple of weeks."

As we walked away, Bubba leaned closer. "I thought you were going to turn it down."

"I considered it. But as long as we have a contract, I think we'll be fine. Oh, and Heather? Make the down payment substantial. I don't want to have bad blood between family." I felt Nic's questions but ignored them. I didn't know what Uncle Arthur was doing. What they'd told Heather on the original call versus what he'd told me today was two different stories. But which one was the lie?

I guess I didn't really care, as long as Cayce's Treasures got paid for the work.

Tessa wasn't outside the shop when we returned. Mel, Jennifer, and Lilac were all talking with customers. Heather and I sat at one of the dining room tables and made notes on the new project. Working together like this, made the designing more fun. I grabbed a sheet of paper and wrote SOLD on top of it, then walked over to the table I'd planned to use for the dining room. Then I went into our inventory system and changed the status of the dining room set and the chandelier to pending with the Ardronic Project listed.

There were a few other items I wanted to save but that could wait until Heather drew up the budget and we had a final contract. By the time I'd finished that, most of the staff and customers had left. Mel came over and dropped into the chair next to me.

"That was a crazy day." She had brought over the calendar and project listing. "So are you taking this new project?"

"Sounds like it, as long as my uncle agrees to the price. I'd love to work on that house. It's perfect and I already have a vision in my head on what it could be. Of course, we still have the Clayborne Estate project that will last for months once we get started next week. I think with Will, we can have at most, three large projects going, maybe four. I'd like to have one person head up each project and call the rest of us in when they need us. So we'd all be working on projects at the beginning and probably at the end when the time crunches." I closed my folder on the laptop, then closed the laptop. Mel was avoiding eye contact. "Okay, what's wrong? Something with what I said."

"How well do you know this Will guy?" Mel took a folder from the back of the calendar she'd brought over.

"He was in school with me. I know he has talent, but other than that, not much. You're going to tell me his references didn't check out." I didn't want to hear this mostly because I hated interviewing. I wanted a full staff by snapping my fingers. I guess that only happens in the movies.

"He has a felony on his record. From Seattle. He robbed a convenience store, which is probably why he dropped out of school. It wasn't violent, but he did time. It was after that he came to New Orleans and started working for the auction house. I don't think they pulled a full background. I wouldn't have based on the way he looks and acts. But we have a policy to run one on all employees and you asked for it." Mel handed me the folder. "I'd still hire him, but I think you need to make that decision. We'll have to inform the insurance company if we do. It could increase our rates."

"Start a business, they said. It will be fun, they said. Instead, this is crazy." I took the folder and put it into my tote. I wondered if the police record was what had bothered me about Will.

"Are you ready to head home?" Bubba stood next to me with my jacket. "I can go get Lilac from your office."

"I'll go. I need to get Alexander's folder anyway." I pulled myself up and headed to the elevator. "You two get everything ready to close. We're done for the day."

9

We were waiting for dinner to be delivered, so I sat in my office and reviewed Alexander's file one last time before I decided if I was going to hand it to Charles Boone or take it back to our resident monster hunter. All the victims had been young and pretty. And at least Skye had a little bit of talent for deception. I went over to my bookshelf and scrolled through the books I'd collected over the years. I had an eclectic collection. Design books from my college years, non-fiction about Seattle and New Orleans, fiction I'd loved or still needed to find time to read, and my share of the collection from my parents.

That was the section I was drawn to search for today. I'd read a book or been told a story about a gift collector when I was a kid. The story had terrified me and I had slept with the lights on for a month after my first encounter with the notion. A monster who killed others for their talents. So he or she could be more powerful.

My mom had explained that power like mine tended to be strong in kids and tap out when they were young adults unless we had the true gift. Then it just got stronger. But the ones who were just touched with the gift, let the world of reality take most of that power away as they grew up into adults. To be honest, I was probably hoping I only had the touch of a gift, and moving to Seattle was a way to deplete it. When I left home after high school, all I wanted to be was normal.

That didn't happen. Although being away from New Orleans had dampened my gift, it had still been there when I returned. And when Grandma Andrews passed on the family gift to add to my own, my abilities had gone through the roof. Which is one of the reasons I appreciated the warded house. As an introvert, I needed time to recharge. If I had to deal with lost souls twenty-four-seven, I'd probably go crazy.

I pulled the book down off the shelf and sat down on the couch to read the story again. In the margin of the story, my mother or someone had written a note. The ink was faded but it appeared to be a name. Had my mother been aware of a power-sucking monster in the area even back then? I took the book over to the desk and looked to see if I had something to magnify the faded entry.

After searching my desk, I leaned back in my chair in frustration. Why didn't I own one of those cool magnifying glasses? I was a horrible mystery solver since I didn't even have the right tools.

Bubba stuck his head into the office. "Hey, dinner's here. Lilac ordered Chinese and it looks like there's one of everything. So come eat."

"I'm just trying to read this. Can you make it out?" I pointed to the page and pushed the book toward him.

"Make out what?" He studied the book and then met my gaze. "The story?"

"No, the word written right there. It's so faded, I can't see it." I tapped the margin where the writing was.

"There's nothing there." Bubba pulled out his phone. "At least not what I can see. Use the photo app to blow up the area. Maybe it's spelled so only you can see it?"

I took his phone and enlarged the word. It was written in cursive and just said, *Art*. I handed him back his phone. "Thanks for the idea. But you really can't see that?"

"No. Not even when you blew it up. All I saw was the cream color of the paper." He put his phone away. "Ready to eat?"

I nodded and stood. This could wait and I was starving. "Thanks for not thinking I'm crazy."

"Eddie, that train left the station after I met Harry. I know you have other senses than I do, so now I just go with the flow." He smiled at me and for the first time in a long time, I didn't feel different because of my talents.

Bubba accepted me as I was. The full me. Not just the public face I used with normal people. Maybe I was normal with a touch of special. I followed him down the hall. "You're amazing."

The smell of shrimp fried rice and kung pao chicken made my stomach growl as soon as we walked into the kitchen where Lilac had set up the spread on the table in the breakfast nook. We ate more meals here than in the fancy dining room. I guess we were a lot like families all over the country.

Lilac looked up as she was setting plates on the table. "Great, you're here. I was about to steal an egg roll. I'm starving."

A thought hit me. "Lilac, after dinner, I need to show you something. Don't let me forget."

"Okay," Lilac sat and opened one of the delivery boxes. "That's not ominous at all. This is Broccoli Beef."

"Mine." Bubba held out his hand. "Does anyone else want some?"

Lilac dished out some onto her plate before she handed it to me. "I love Chinese takeout nights. I get a little bit of everything."

As dinner progressed, I watched Lilac. She seemed better today, not as overwhelmed with grief. However, since I'd recently lost my grandmother, I knew one minute of time could be misleading. But Bubba was keeping the conversation light, which I appreciated.

After dinner, Lilac met me in my office, and I showed her the page. She didn't see anything either. So, the word wasn't tied to a person with psychic powers. Maybe instead, it was tied to my bloodline. Could it be a message from my mother?"

I put the book in my tote, hoping to get to talk to Nic tomorrow. I felt like all I'd been doing for the last few days was dodging attacks and surprises. I still had no idea why Skye had been killed, although I had a feeling it was tied to the work she was doing. Maybe if I'd ask, Uncle Arthur would tell me if Skye was part of his crew. Or, more likely, he'd pull the design contract from me and never talk to me again. I'd wait until I at least had the deposit.

Family. It was a pain.

It turned out that I didn't have to wait to talk to Nic because he showed up just as I had curled up on the sofa with Dr. Dexter and a book.

Bubba let him in and I could hear the tension in Nic's voice as he came through the foyer. When he found me in the living room, he stared. "What on earth are you thinking?"

I set the book down. I didn't think this was going to be a short conversation. "Nice to see you, have a chair."

He glared at me but took his jacket off and sat down. Bubba still stood in the doorway. "Sorry, it's been a crazy day. So why are you working for Uncle Arthur?"

"Because he asked me to remodel a house? That's what I do for a living, remember?" I caught Bubba's gaze and shook my head. He didn't need to be listening to me fight with my brother.

Bubba took the hint and went back into the kitchen where he and Lilac had cleared dinner off the table. They had started a board game. I'd played one-night last week and had been wiped off the table early so now I just kept my evenings free for time with my book or working on a design for one of my customers.

"He's trying to pit us against each other, you know that." Nic rubbed his face. He did look tired.

"Since we both know what he's doing, his game isn't going to work." I leaned forward. "Nic, you have to trust me. I'm just remodeling a house for him. I'm not swearing allegiance to his plan to take over the company."

"You're right. I'm beat and when I heard this from my secretary, it set me off." He stood. "Annamae has dinner waiting, I better get home."

I stood as well. "One more thing. Can you look at something for me?"

He followed me into my office, and I showed him the faint 'Art' in the margin of the book.

"So what's the problem. Mom used to write in these books all the time. I found one where she made a shopping list. She wasn't careful with her reading material." He turned the book over and shook his head. "These are fairy tales. You or I might have written that as a kid."

"But you see it, don't you?" I took the book and turned it back to the page. "What does it mean?"

"What do you mean, can I see it? It's right there." Now my brother looked at me like I was crazy. "Are you feeling all right?"

"Hey Bubba, come tell me what the word in the book says." I called out to the kitchen.

A groan sounded. "Eddie, I told you, I can't see any word in your book's margin. And neither can Lilac. Can you leave us alone? I'm about to wipe her out of the northern territories."

"Am not," Lilac responded.

Nic turned to me. "They can't see it?"

I shook my head as I studied the word. "No. Neither one of them. I would have called over Alexander, but I thought I'd check with you first. I think it has something to do with our bloodline."

"Possible. I've heard of messages being sent down from one generation to the next using an ink that no one but a relative could see, but I've never come across anything." He pulled out his phone and took a picture. Then he looked at the picture and swore. "And it's invisible again. What is this?"

"Funny. I could see the word through my camera when I blew it up, but I didn't think about taking a picture of it. I think it's a message from Mom." I tapped my finger on the desk. "What art works do we have at the compound. Anything that shows a monster?"

"I'll ask Annamae. I know there's more than what's been displayed because she changes things out now and then. Maybe you should come stay with me this week." Nic stood and put back on his jacket.

"I'm in a warded house. I don't think I've got anything to worry about." I pointed to the wall that butted up against Alexander's condo. "Besides, I've got a monster hunter living next door."

Laughter came from the kitchen and I smiled in that direction. "And I have them."

"Well, I'm going to talk with Annamae and see what paintings we have in stock and where. You may have to come by this weekend and go through them to see what Mom was trying to say. It might be important."

"I think it is important." I followed him to the door. "I'm glad Trenton is driving. You look like you could sleep for a month."

"As soon as the rest of the board leaves, I will. I spent today in meetings explaining the same thing over and over. Which I could have done once at a board meeting if they hadn't gotten spooked over the death." He reached down and rubbed Dr. Dexter's ears. "You keep Eddie safe, okay?"

Dr. Dexter barked a response, which made me laugh. As Nic was leaving, I touched his arm. "I think Skye's death is connected with Uncle Arthur's other business."

"Which is another reason I don't like the idea of you designing his new house. Anyway, stay safe and keep Bubba close. I don't like this situation at all." He pulled my sweater together in the front. "You should be more discerning about your clientele."

"If I didn't do business with anyone attached to the family business, my customer pool would shrink by ninety percent. You have quite the corporate reach. Even the Clayborne Estate owner is a board member."

Nic sighed. "I know, I sent her your way when she asked about designers. I guess I can't gripe when I'm part of the problem."

As he left, I stared out at the now empty street. Who would have sent the ghosts to attack Lilac and why? Did she know something she didn't realize about Skye's death? Or was it someone from my past who was making a statement? Okay, so someone from my family. I sighed as I closed the front door and locked it. Even with a cheating fiancé and a boring job, Seattle had been so quiet compared to my life here.

Laughter came out from the kitchen where Bubba and Lilac had resumed playing their game. The house glowed with life. Fluffy, Bubba's cat was sitting on the back of the couch, watching me. I went over and pulled her into my lap. "I know. Sometimes quiet isn't what you want out of life. This is pretty special, isn't it?"

Fluffy yawned and curled up to go to sleep. I'd take that as agreement.

FRIDAY MORNING, I got a delivery at the house before work. I opened the box and found an antique mantel clock. A card was tucked into the pink wrapping. I read the card aloud, "Eddie, it occurs to me I haven't sent you a housewarming gift yet. I hope your time here in New Orleans envelopes you in sweet memories. Uncle Arthur."

Bubba pulled on his suit jacket. "Your uncle sent that? Are we sure it's not a bomb?"

I smiled at the question. "I think he's trying to be a part of my life. Probably not a bomb, but with the contract to redesign his house, it might be a bribe. Or it might have a bug in it and he's listing to us right now. I wish my mom was here to talk to. She was good at sorting through the chaff for the wheat."

He held out his hand for the clock. "Do you mind if I have it checked out with the security guys? I'd hate to have a hidden camera or microphone found in it after it was too late."

"You're always looking for the downside." I put the clock back in the box and handed it to him. "But this time, I agree with you. It's lovely and I don't want to see it damaged, but on the other hand, I'm having some trust issues with Uncle Arthur."

"As soon as Danny arrives at the shop, I'll take it to the security team." He folded the box closed.

I started to say something, but he held up a hand. "I'll make sure its confidential. Your uncle won't know. Nic has already gone through the security department to make sure everyone there is loyal to him, not your uncle. But just in case, I'll have it logged as a suspicious item bought by the shop." He glanced at his watch. "Are we ready? I want to take Lilac out first so we can check for a ghost swarm outside the property lines."

"Maybe I should go," I grabbed a jacket.

He shook his head. "I've talked this over with Nic and we both think the swarm yesterday was aimed at you, not Lilac. Don't worry, I won't put her in harm's way. I just can't see the ghosts like the two of you."

"I'll grab my tote and be at the doorway, watching." I hurried to the kitchen and got my coffee and let Lilac know we were leaving. She was just coming inside with Dr. Dexter. "Don't do anything foolish when you go off the property."

"Yes, mother." Lilac grinned at me, then locked the back door. "You have a dinner tonight, right? You don't mind if I have a kegger here while you're gone, do you?"

"You're a horrible brat." I rubbed the dog's head as Lilac filled her own coffee cup. "Do you want to come to the dinner with me? I can bring a plus one."

"I think Bubba's your plus one. We'll be fine here at home. I'm going to order takeout and watch reruns of *Project Runway* I missed while I was on the streets. I need to get caught up on the fashion front." She pulled on a jacket over her neon yellow shirt and torn jeans. Now that Lilac had an income, she'd been shopping the outlet mall and clearance sales for her own style.

"Hey, have you decided on your college program next year?" I didn't want Lilac to think she had to work for me the rest of her life.

She shook her head. "I still can't believe you're paying tuition for me. You know you don't need to do that."

"I know I don't have to pay it. I want to. And it's kind of a family tradition. Just don't be looking at Harvard or Yale or something too far away so I never see you. Like Seattle." I nodded toward the front of the house. "Bubba wants you to go ghost hunting before we leave. If you don't feel comfortable, just let me know and I'll do it."

"I'll do it." She paused as she moved out of the kitchen. "I'll apply for some programs this weekend. I still can't believe how nice you're being to me."

"Lilac, I told you when I brought you home to the compound. You're family now. Not only do you have me, but you also have Nic if you ever need him. And Annamae. Finding someone with your talent is so rare, you need to be supported. I had parents who understood the effects the talents had on me growing up. You didn't. So now it's time to become the person you were always meant to be." I followed her int the hallway, then ducked into my office. The folder that Alexander had given me was on my desk along with the book. I put both in my desk drawer and grabbed my tote. Lilac may not be a child but she didn't need to be seeing what was in that folder.

When I stepped outside and locked the door on a sad looking Dr. Dexter, both Lilac and Bubba were by the sidewalk waiting for me.

"The coast is clear." Bubba held out his arm and I joined them on the sidewalk. As we passed by Alexander's house, I glanced at the front facing windows. He wasn't there. Or at least he wasn't watching us leave. Maybe that was a good thing. I hurried to the streetcar stop and finally relaxed when we climbed aboard.

10

————

Friday morning went by fast especially since I didn't have any appointments scheduled until later that evening when what was left of the board and Nic were expecting me and Bubba for dinner. I let Mel know when I'd be leaving to get ready and she handed me a folder. "What's this?"

"Will's file. His background check including the arrest. There's nothing else that showed up, but you need to make the call on this one before we hire him. I called and let him know that there was an issue with the hiring and that you'd call as soon as you could. He hadn't given notice yet, which is a good thing." Mel had followed me to the elevator but stopped as I got inside. I was working in my office while Bubba went to take the clock to his security team. Danny was already standing near the shop entrance door. Lilac followed me onto the elevator.

"Okay, tell me if I'm overreaching." She held out her laptop. "I'd like to apply for a few and see where I get accepted. Tulane is my top choice, but the design degree would be either graphic or architectural."

"I thought you wanted fashion design." I glanced at the page and handed the tablet back. "I don't care what school you want to go to.

But if you leave the area, you'll need to figure out room and board. You can stay with me until you graduate and get on your feet if you go somewhere you can commute. Or you can get a grant or loans for your room and board. I told you I'd cover tuition and books."

"You don't think Tulane's too expensive?" She flipped to the tuition page.

"You're not listening. Go to the school that you want to graduate from. I've given you your parameters. If you leave the area, you need to figure out room and board. Otherwise, you live with me at the condo." I stepped off the elevator. "I mean, if you want to even go to college?"

"You're kidding right? I thought I'd given up that dream when I left home. I want to go to college and living with you is amazing. I'll need to save for a car though." Lilac bit her bottom lip. "Especially if I go out of the city."

"We'll deal with that when it happens. Nic has several cars available you can use. Maybe even one that doesn't look like you're in the witness protection program and getting dropped off by the FBI or Secret Service."

I set the file on the desk and opened my water to take a drink. When I opened the file, a picture of Will fell out of the file and off the desk. Lilac picked it up.

She went pale. "Who is this?"

"Will Marshall. I'm trying to decide if I'm going to hire him. We went to school together in Seattle." I noticed Lilac's hand shaking as she set the picture down on the desk. "Why?"

"Because that's Skye's boss. The guy who she worked for when she was doing fortunes on the street." She met my gaze. "And he didn't go by Will. His name was something else. I can't remember it right now."

"Are you sure?" I turned the picture toward me. Will looked harder in this picture than he had on Wednesday or back in school. His eyes looked mean. "It's not a good picture of him."

"I think it's a great picture of him. He always looked like that. Hungry. Like he wanted to cut out my heart and eat it. Skye knew he scared me so she kept my talent from him. But I always thought he could see into my head. That he knew I had a secret. After she started working with him, Skye introduced me to Kirk and he got me the job here. I didn't like her being around him, but she said she would be fine. Which she wasn't. He didn't kill her, did he?"

"I don't know." I needed to talk to Bubba.

I pulled out my phone, but as soon as I did, he came into the office to let me know he was back.

"I had to leave the clock there, but we'll have a report and hopefully the clock back on Monday." Bubba leaned against the door. He stared at Lilac, then at me. "Okay, what did I miss?"

I explained about Will and Lilac gave him all the information she had. I handed him the folder. "Do you need to go back to the security office?"

He shook his head. "I'll make the calls from here. Just let me know if either of you see this guy again. I think you're going to have to do more interviews, Eddie."

"I was afraid you were going to say that." I watched him leave and noticed Lilac had curled up in her chair. She looked rattled. "Anyway, why don't you work on making a pros and cons worksheet for your college choices. Figure out what program you want, then search out the best schools. If they're here, put them on the list. If not, let's just narrow down the choices by the end of the weekend so you can get applications sent in. You're running out of time."

Lilac curled her tablet to her chest as she stood. "I can't believe you're this calm about Will."

"We don't know that he did anything, except get Skye involved in a shady business." I tried to ease her fears. "Let's let Bubba find out what is going on and then we can make a decision on Will."

She nodded. "I'm heading downstairs to work near Mel's desk. She said she'd make me an Excel spreadsheet I could use to compare the colleges."

I watched her leave the office and hoped my friend Will hadn't been involved in Skye's death. Maybe he just looked like Skye's boss. Like in those shows where the evil twin is doing things and the good twin gets blamed. Except Will had told me in Seattle he didn't have any siblings.

I leaned back in my chair and closed my eyes, hoping for a favorable outcome. Then I sat up and pulled out some paper. No matter what, I had projects to complete and a business to run. I started a to do list and started delegating tasks.

After I had a plan using the people and time I had, I felt better. The Clayborne Estate project would be headed by Heather. She could hire on labor as she needed and had good contacts in the area. I'd take on Uncle Arthur's house. And Mel would focus on the business. I sent out an email with all of this detailed out to everyone on staff. I didn't mention Will, either his possible hiring or inability to be part of the team.

Mel came up at lunch and asked if I wanted to eat with the group or she could send up a plate. They'd ordered in soups and salads from a local deli I loved.

"I'll come down." I saved the drafting file I'd been working on for the Burgundy Street Project – I'd decided to stop calling it Uncle Arthur's house, at least for my project records. I closed the paper file on my desk where I'd kept all my notes. I should have a budget proposal to share with a contract sometime next week. I wanted to get him committed before he decided this was a bad idea. A concept that was already floating around in Nic's head and at time's in mine. However, right now, I needed projects for Cayce's Treasures. Projects I could show other prospective clients. So if I had to work with the devil, I was going to do it. At least for a few jobs.

"What's going on with Will," Mel asked when we were in the elevator. "I saw the email."

"Honestly, I don't know. I need more information. And there's a possibility that he might have a history with Lilac. If that's true, I don't want to make her uncomfortable by hiring him." I saw the look Mel gave me. "Let's just see where the investigation goes, then we'll make a decision after that."

"It's your playhouse." Mel pointed to the conference room where most of the staff were eating.

"That's what they tell me," I laughed as I started, but then she turned back to the sales floor. "Aren't you coming?"

"I'm watching the store. Then Jennifer will replace me so I can eat. Danny's on the floor too and Bubba's eating. We've got this covered. Staff meals are one thing I can take off your plate without you having any concerns." She shooed me toward the conference room. "Oh, and Heather's there. She says she needs to talk to you about the Clayborne assignment."

"I kind of expected her to show up today." I waved at Mel and headed to the conference room to eat and calm Heather down. She would be amazing at lead designer. She just didn't know it yet.

When it was time to leave, I pulled Lilac aside. "Do you want to go with me? Or should I have Danny bring you home?"

Lilac blushed so hard her face looked like pink neon. "I can find my way home. The streetcar isn't that far away."

"We're kind of in a strange place here and Nic and I would feel better if you had an escort. So either its leave with me and Bubba or Danny will bring you home at five. Your choice." Lilac liked Nic and I knew she didn't want to disappoint him. Me, she could disappoint since she knew I adored her like a sister.

"You're just punishing me for taking off the other day to try to find Skye's killer." Lilac quickly responded.

"You think?" I stared her down and to my surprise, she blinked first.

She nodded. "Okay, I'll admit, that was dumb. I was just so upset. And when the ghost told me that I could help, I didn't think about it. I'll go home at five. With Danny."

"Okay, I'll probably be gone or close to leaving, so no boys in the house. Not even Danny or our handsome neighbor."

"Neither of whom are boys." Lilac smiled and I knew she was over her snit. "I'll probably be asleep when you get back so if you and Bubba want to hang out in the living room, *talking*, I wouldn't know."

Now it was my turn to blush. I grabbed my tote and jacket and turned toward the front door where Bubba was waiting. "I'll see you later."

~

We were ready to leave by five and the dinner was back across town, so I followed Bubba to the waiting limo out front. I pulled the overflowing skirt of the dress Annamae had sent over for me to give Bubba room to sit. "We should have just stayed at work and got dressed there."

He adjusted the tie on his tuxedo. "That's what I like about you, Eddie. Most girls would love the primping they get to do for an event like this. You just treat it like it's an annoyance."

"Well, thank you? I think that was a compliment." I adjusted the sweetheart top of the light blue dress that seemed to have glitter weaved into the fabric. "I hated my prom and this is worse, since there's a meal attached where I have to be social with more than one person. We should have had them to the compound for dinner. That was the original plan."

"Then Annamae would have had to cook. You know she won't let a caterer in her kitchen." Bubba took out his phone and snapped a picture of me.

"What are you doing?" I asked, self-consciously.

"I don't want to forget this night. You look amazing." He went to put away his phone, but I stopped him. I pulled him closer and aimed the phone at both of us.

"Then let's get us both in the shot because you look pretty good yourself." I smiled at the camera as he took several shots. "Send me those, okay?"

As we drove up to the hotel where the dinner was being held, another limo was in front of us. Aunt Franny climbed out and adjusted her dress. A younger man took her arm and as they went into the lobby together, he whispered something in her ear to make her blush and giggle.

"Your aunt likes her men young," Bubba said.

A pit formed in the bottom of my stomach. "I didn't realize she'd even be here. I hope this doesn't turn into a screaming match. We might be leaving before the main course is served."

The driver met my gaze in the rear-view mirror. "I'll hang close by, just in case."

Bubba got out and did a visual sweep of the street. Then he opened my door. I mumbled thanks to the driver and stepped out, my dress catching in the soft wind.

Bubba smiled as he held out his hand. "Like I said, you look amazing."

"That's true. I don't think I've seen you in a dress like that since Junior Prom." Detective Charles Boone stepped out of the hotel and greeted me. "I take it you're here for the big dinner your brother's company is putting on?"

"Ardronic Enterprises, yes. It's not just my brother's company. He's just the CEO." I kissed Boone on the cheek. "What are you doing here?"

"Talking to your uncle. It's been hard to reach him. He swears he doesn't have his own street group doing fortunes for the tourists. Although, rumor is, he's running the con." Boone glanced back at the doorway and then at me. "Did Lilac remember anything else about her friend's employers?"

I shook my head. "We've been trying to keep her busy so she doesn't have to think about it. Is there a funeral scheduled?"

Boone sighed. "She was a street kid. Her mom is in rehab and dad's out of the picture. We'll be releasing the body soon so if you want to do something for her before the county takes responsibility, have a funeral home call the morgue. I hate it when the kids don't have anyone to take them home."

"I'll find someone. She deserves to have a proper burial." I knew Skye's soul was already gone from this world, but Lilac still needed a chance to say goodbye to her friend. "I'll have them reach out by Monday if that's not too late."

"You're a class act, Eddie." Boone's phone rang. He glanced at the display. "I've got to take this. Have a nice night, Eddie. Beauregard."

As Boone walked away, he picked up the phone. "Nothing. I just finished talking to him. What about..."

I couldn't hear anything else as he was out of earshot by then.

"Remind me to call Annamae and have her find a place in the family section of the graveyard. And I need to know who the family uses. Weird, I should know this since Grandma just died, but I didn't pay attention."

"You were grieving, not fact finding." Bubba took my arm. "I never thought I'd say this, but I have to agree with Boone on one thing. You are a class act."

I shook my head as we stepped up into the lobby area. "I'm just doing what's right. Let's go mingle so we can get out of here. I want to kick off these shoes already and put on slippers."

We walked through the large room, greeting and talking to board members as we moved. Finally, we ran into Aunt Franny. I tensed for the heated exchange. "Good evening, Auntie."

"Auntie? That's a little informal, but I guess it will do." Her gaze swept the room. "So many people here. You and Nic are doing a great job at building up your supporters. I take it your Uncle's men left when they heard about the death?"

"The death?" I wasn't giving her anything just in case she was fishing for information.

"Your little friend Lilac's homeless friend. Or didn't she tell you that Skye had been murdered in cold blood?" The look on Aunt Franny's face looked more like glee than condolence.

"I don't think this is the right time to be talking about a murder." I dodged the question.

"Okay, so no murder talk. No talking about your stealing my inheritance. Probably no discussions on what a piece of crap your father was, almost as bad as Arthur." Aunt Franny's eyes burned as her anger increased.

"Here's your wine, my sweet." The young man came back with two glasses of red. He smiled at me. "I'm Todd Wilder. And you must be dear Franny's sister? You look so much alike."

"I'm Eddie Cayce, Franny's my aunt." I shook the offered hand. "She's my mother's older sister."

Aunt Franny hissed at me and as Todd put his hand on her arm, Bubba stepped between us. He moved me a few steps back from my aunt. "We need to find your brother and let him know we've arrived. Nice to meet you, Todd."

When we were on the other side of the room, I breathed again. My aunt was crazy and I was poking the bear. What was I thinking? "Sorry and thanks for pulling me out of that."

"Honestly, I didn't think you were going to be the one to throw the first verbal punch. But that was a good one. Todd set you up for that slap nicely." Bubba chuckled as he pointed out Nic. "I think you're needed over there."

"Todd's an idiot." I moved to my brother's side and kissed him on the cheek. "Sorry we're late."

"You wouldn't have been if you hadn't stopped to antagonize Aunt Franny. What, did her young man steal your after-nap cookies?" Nic smiled and greeted a board member who was walking by on the way to the bar.

"She's just mean." I glanced around the room. Most of these people had also been at the housewarming party I'd held a few months ago. They were loyal to Nic and through him, to me as well. If we couldn't feel safe here, there was no place we would. Although Aunt Franny and Uncle Arthur were like having the foxes in the hen house. And we were feeding them an amuse-bouche before their real dinner.

Us.

11

As we found our seats, I noticed Will Marshall coming into the room. He was dressed in a tuxedo, and he scanned the room. He didn't notice me at all, in fact, he looked right through me. He found who he was looking for and made a beeline to the bar area. As I watched, he put an arm around my aunt and kissed her.

Todd had just come back with another glass of wine. He squealed as he saw Will kiss Aunt Franny. I thought I heard him say, "You had your chance."

It was like watching a movie. Both men thought that they were there with my aunt. I assumed that they were under a compulsion spell. I continued to watch as testosterone flew with the angry words. Finally, the hotel security team took both men outside.

I turned to Bubba. "That was weird."

"Do you want me to go find out what was going on?" He watched as Aunt Franny sat down at the table and chatted with her neighbor like nothing out of the ordinary had happened.

I nodded. I needed to find out how Will knew my aunt. And if it had anything to do with him wanting a job at my shop. Or if his connection was just coincidence. "Thanks, Bubba."

He stepped over to one of the security guards by the doors. Whatever he'd said, one of them left with Bubba and I turned back to the table. I had been set with Nic and two of the board members and their spouses. We had seven at our table since Nic had added a spot for Bubba. Turning to my brother, I asked, "No Esmeralda tonight?"

He frowned at me since both of the board members had paused their conversations to hear Nic's answer. "She couldn't get away from South Cove. She has responsibilities there."

Eliza Clayborne patted Nic's arm. "Jeremy felt the same way about my occupation. He hated going to these types of events alone. It's so nice that you're supporting her and her adventures. Although it would be nice to see Esmeralda once in a while. She's such a vibrant conversationalist."

Peter Miles, the other board member at our table, slapped Nic on the back as he stood to get another drink from the bar. "If you don't control them early, they'll control you all your life."

"Peter," his wife gasped. "I can't believe you said that."

Peter winked at Nic. "See what I mean?"

The people at the table laughed as the first course was brought and Peter hurried back with a glass of wine for his wife. Bubba slipped in beside me. "Sorry for my tardiness. Just checking on something."

I took a sip of cold gazpacho soup. "Everything okay?"

He nodded, then dropped his voice. "Apparently your aunt had invited two dates for tonight. She went out and cleared up the matter, sending Will home. She and Todd are seated at the table by the door."

"I can't believe Aunt Franny even knows Will." I glanced over to where they were sitting. My aunt was watching me but turned her head as I met her gaze. "Something's going on."

Uncle Arthur was seated at another table with a date. She was beautiful and I was certain, this was Tamera, his girlfriend who lived in Jamaica. And as soon as I got the house remodeled, Tamera would be making New Orleans her home. Or part time home. I couldn't imagine leaving the beach. He smiled at me, then leaned over to whisper something in Tamera's ear. Her eyes lit up as she found me in the crowd and smiled at me with a tiny wave. Uncle Arthur might be keeping her secret from the family, but it was obvious, he wasn't keeping us from her. I made a mental note to go introduce myself after the dinner.

When the final course, a blueberry bread pudding with a rum sauce was served with coffee, Nic stood and buttoned his suit jacket. It was time for a speech even though the board meeting event had been scaled down to just the dinner.

He went to the platform and pulled out note cards for his speech. He smiled and leaned into the microphone. "My friends..."

Smoke filled the room and people stood, moving quickly toward the door. Bubba had my arm. "Fire, we need to get you out."

"But Nic," I turned toward the stage but he was gone from the podium as the smoke thickened, I saw him on my other side.

"Hurry, Eddie. This isn't random." Nic didn't bother to whisper. Whoever had attacked had one thing in mind. To kill him or me or both. I tripped and went down, and Bubba fell as well. People were still pushing their way out of the ballroom and my foot got stepped on. A hand grabbed my arm and pulled me up. I looked up to thank Bubba, but Will was there instead.

He pushed me to the right and instead of heading outside the hotel, I found myself in a hallway being drug to a side exit. "What are you doing," I coughed and tried to scream when he didn't answer.

I grabbed a doorway, which made him slow as I found myself pulled between him and the grip I held on the door.

"Let go. I need to get you outside where they won't find you." Will muttered as he yanked on my arm.

"What is taking you so long?" My aunt stepped inside the exit door, waving us toward her.

A young boy materialized between us. "You shouldn't go with him. He has a gun."

"I know that, but I can't hold on much longer," I told the ghost. "Help me."

He flashed out for a second, but when he came back, there were more ghosts with him. They surrounded Will and his eyes widened. Then just before my fingers tore from the doorframe, he let go, holding his hands to his face.

"Go away, you're not real," he screamed to the ghost mob.

"Will, don't listen to them. Just bring her to me. Everything will be okay if you bring her to me." Aunt Franny pleaded from the doorway.

"No! Stop it, you're not real." Will cried as he reached for his gun with one hand, waving the ghosts away with the other. I didn't think he even heard what Aunt Franny said. He started shooting into the ghost mist and I ran in the opposite direction, back toward the smoke. If he couldn't see me, maybe he couldn't shoot me.

I felt a bullet fly by my face and hit the wall just before I turned right, back into the smoke-filled hallway toward the hotel's main lobby and the outside doors.

A guard took my arm and helped me toward the exit as Bubba ran up to me. He looked me over as his breathing slowed. "Where were you?"

"Will grabbed me," I nodded toward the exit. "Let's get out of here before Aunt Franny shows up with a machine gun."

Bubba took my arm and I held on tight as we hurried toward the doorway. The other guard went back inside the smoke. Once we were outside, I felt Bubba turn like he was going to go after Will, but I kept pulling him toward the street. "Don't, he has a gun."

Bubba stopped fighting me. But then he pulled me aside to where a security guard stood holding the doors open and watching the crowd leave. He looked at me. "Tell him what you just told me."

Relaying my attempted kidnapping, I saw the guard pull out his cell. He talked to someone to check the residential hallway by the exit. "We'll find him. Please wait outside until we determine if the fire has been put out and it's safe to return."

Bubba pressed a business card into the guard's hand. "Call me with what you find. I'm getting her out of here."

The guard was about to argue, but Bubba didn't give him time. He put his arm around me and we moved out of the hotel's entryway and onto the sidewalk. A car was waiting near the entrance and Nic opened a door, waving at us from inside. "Come on, we've been waiting for you. What did you do, go fix your hair?"

I fell into the seat and as Bubba got in and closed the door, he called out to the driver. "Get us out of here."

I felt fingers on my shoulder. Bubba was turning me toward him. The smoke on his hand made my neck sting. I shrugged his hand off. "Stop it. I'm fine."

He shook his head. "Actually, you're not. It looks like a bullet skimmed you as it went by. If you had been a little taller or he'd aimed lower, you might have been killed. Did you get shot anywhere else?"

Now Nic and Bubba both were scanning my dress for blood stains. Standing for them to look at my back, I fell back into my seat when the car hit a bump. "I'm okay. I would know if I had been shot."

"Except you were and you didn't," Nic pointed out. "We need to get her to the hospital. I'm calling Boone."

"No, I need to get home. If Will gets away, he or Aunt Franny might go after Lilac to get to me." I took Bubba's offered handkerchief and pressed it to my shoulder. I winced at the now stinging pain, but I didn't want to get blood on this dress. The cleaners would already have a problem with the smoke damage.

Nic stared at me while he held the phone.

The driver asked, "Sir?"

He pointed at me. "You better not have been hurt anywhere else. Go ahead and head to Ms. Cayce's house."

I leaned back in the seat and took a breath. Then I coughed again. The wound on my shoulder reacted with a sharper pain. "Anyone have something to drink?"

"Water? Or something harder?" Nic opened the bar in the back seat.

"Do you have a Coke? And maybe a shot of something soft?" I didn't want to close my eyes as I felt myself reacting to the shock of the night's activities. I needed alcohol for the pain and sugar to boost my energy. All I wanted to do was sleep and that wasn't happening until I was home and knew Lilac was safe.

"Of course." He handed Bubba the bottle of Coke and then opened a small bottle of what appeared to be a Hurricane rum mix. "Drink this first."

"Are you sure it has rum in it?" I squinted to try to read the bottle's ingredients.

He looked at me like I was an idiot. "I keep these here for guests when they come into New Orleans for business. It's a nice welcome and the rum calms them down."

I downed the tiny bottle. "One more."

He handed me a second bottle and after I downed it, I could feel the energy from the fruit juice waking me up. And the rum didn't hurt either. I took the bottle of Coke, Bubba had opened and took a few sips, then put the lid back on.

"What happened?" Bubba looked at Nic. "Could you see anything?"

"The smoke came from behind me. I'm thinking either the same man set it off and then ran to the edge to grab Eddie or there were two of them." Nic held up his hand and started talking in his phone when Boone answered.

"Tell him it was Will Michell and Aunt Franny. I have his employment file if he needs more information. I think he gave us the correct information as Mel was able to find his prison record." I took another sip of my Coke. "This is Aunt Franny's doing. He thought he was with her tonight. Maybe she had him under a compulsion spell."

Boone's voice sounded from the phone speaker. "You had me right up to the woo woo spell idea. So this Will, he applied for a job with you?"

"Yes. I knew him in Seattle. We went to school together. Or we did freshman year. Then he got arrested for a robbery. Lilac says he was the one Skye worked for, not Uncle Arthur. Or maybe he was just her handler. I don't know." I leaned toward the phone Nic was now holding out. "And he kissed my Aunt Franny tonight before dinner."

"And that proves?" Boone asked.

"She knew him. And she shouldn't. He was from Seattle, not New Orleans. He said he was working for the auction house. I think he was going to kill me but the ghosts attacked him and made him let go of me in the hallway." I could feel Boone's lack of belief through the telephone connection. "I know how it sounds, but it's true. And my aunt was waiting at the exit for him to drag me out. I heard her call to him."

Boone's sigh was long and loud. "So you slipped away from him and then what happened?"

Boone didn't want to talk about ghosts or spells. "He started shooting. I guess he hit me because I have a scratch on my shoulder."

"You're going to the hospital? I'll check at the hotel first, then come over."

"I'm not going to the hospital. I'll be at home." My shoulder twinged again and I sucked in air, trying not to react to the pain. I didn't want Nic to change our destination.

Nic took back the phone. "We think this Will guy tried to kill Eddie for our Aunt Franny. Maybe you could find him or her and see if that's true. And, if Lilac's right, he might be the one you should be looking at for Skye's death as well."

After Nic finished talking to Boone, the driver pulled up in front of my house. I took out the keys from my beaded purse and handed them to Bubba. "Lilac better not have gone anywhere."

Bubba chuckled and stepped out of the car. Then he leaned back inside to put his arm around my good side and help me get out onto the sidewalk. We didn't stay out there long. He almost carried me as we hurried to the property line inside the wards. We waited by the door for Nic to join us. No use taking any chances. The ghosts from the hotel had helped me tonight, but I knew my aunt had power with them as well.

The door to the house flew open and Lilac stood inside, watching us. "You're home early," she called as she held Dr. Dexter's collar.

Relief filled me as I hurried over to the door. Nic and Bubba could follow us. "I'm so glad you're here."

"Where else would I be. I'm kind of on house arrest, remember." She reached out and touched the handkerchief that was now blooming with red blood. "What happened?"

"I need to sit down." I moved inside and felt Nic on one side and Bubba on the other. Lilac shut the door behind them and I heard the sound of locks being engaged. "Take me to the living room."

After they got me situated on the couch, I took another sip of my Coke. I looked at Nic. "So is Boone coming here?"

"Yes, after he checks in at the hotel. Maybe your ghosts will have Will wrapped up and secured for him." Nic sat next to me and took the handkerchief off. "We need to clean and bandage this. And see if you have any pain killers."

Bubba nodded. "I'll get what we need."

As he took off, I looked at Lilac. "Can you go into my office and take Will's file out of the tote bag. I need to give it to Boone. There's another file in my left-hand desk drawer. Don't open it, just bring it here. And call Mel and tell her we aren't hiring Will and he is dangerous."

"Sure." Lilac took off.

Bubba came back with a ton of bandages, hydroperoxide and a bottle of Tylenol. He took three of the pills and handed them to me. "It won't stop the pain, but it might dull it. You should see a doctor."

"We'll see." I took the pills and finished the Coke. I was beginning to feel normal although I still tasted smoke in my mouth. Lilac was standing in the doorway with the files. "Just sit those on the table. Detective Boone needs them. He'll be here soon. And stay away from that guy if you see him. Did you call Mel?"

Lilac stepped in and set the files on the coffee table, keeping the picture. "I remember his name now. The one that he went by when I knew him. That's Steve, Skye's boyfriend. He's the one who set her up with the job. The one she told me to stay away from."

I took the picture, looked at it and then handed it back. "That's Will. Call Mel and tell her we're not hiring him."

A knock on the door interrupted their discussion over Will or Steve. The guy seemed to like being unknowable.

"I'll get it," Lilac jumped up from the floor where both Dr. Dexter and Fluffy had been curled next to her.

"It's probably Boone." I said as I adjusted from where I was sitting.

The wound was bandaged, but I still wanted to go upstairs and take a short bath to clean the smell of smoke off me. I'd probably have to burn my dress but I'd take it to the cleaners and hope.

"I'm going to go make more coffee. Anyone else want some?" Bubba asked as he stepped out. "Then I'm going to change into clean jeans and a shirt. I'll still smell like a campfire, but I won't look like a monkey."

"You don't look like a monkey. Besides, I know you're just going so you won't have to talk to Boone." I called after him.

"Not entirely true. We do need more coffee." He called back, making me smile.

Nic shook his head. "Those two are still hold a grudge from high school. That's commitment."

"High school holds some of the most traumatic memories," Alexander Morgan said as he walked into the living room. "Sorry to bother you but I had a feeling you were all still up and that something had broken in the case."

CHAPTER 12

"You had a feeling?" I stared at him when he finally walked around the couch where I didn't have to move my head. Alexander Morgan tended to slip around the legal side of things, at least from what I could tell. And now, I was beginning to have my own feeling and it was bad. "Don't tell me I need to sweep the house for bugs."

"You had a termite inspection when you bought the condo." Alexander smiled as he sat down in a chair.

"That's not the kind of bugs I'm talking about and you know it." I stared at him.

"Okay, honesty. I can do that. Your lights are on. I saw you come home from your event and wanted to stop in. I do not have electronic surveillance on your condo except the security system that just happens shows your front door and our back yard. I'm just being careful. I have a lot of valuable antiques," he said as he pointedly looked around the living room. "As you do as well."

"Okay, point taken." I was still going to have Bubba sweep the house for bugs. I couldn't believe that I hadn't thought of it before. "So how can I help you tonight."

"Tell me what's going on with the case." He leaned back in the chair and studied me. Then he sat up, noticing my bandage. "Oh, dear. Are you alright?"

"I'm fine. Someone tried to kidnap me and when I called on the ghosts to help, he shot randomly and grazed my shoulder." I knew at least Alexander would believe the ghost part.

"Why would he kidnap you?"

I explained what had happened and the fact my aunt was involved. Finally, I added, "I'm not sure if they were looking to kill me or just steal my power somehow."

"I'm not sure those are two different scenarios. The power has to have a vessel when the host body terminates. Either it's contained in a jar or vial, or it goes into a willing new host." He picked up the employment file I'd made on Will and quickly read the information. Then he sat it down. "Thank you. I should be able to solve this ongoing problem now."

"You think Will killed Skye as well." I stated the obvious. "Oh, and Lilac knows him as Steve."

He nodded as he stood. "I do. But I think there's a stronger personality manipulating this man. It may be your aunt. I'll find him and see what I can determine. We may close this case sooner than I believed."

"What happens to Will when you close the case? If I'm right, he was under a compulsion. He didn't know what he was doing." I had seen Will's eyes as he tried to pull me away from the doorway. The man I knew wasn't there. Or at least he wasn't driving the tractor, so to speak.

"He will be dealt with. I don't know if you understand, a man can't be compelled to do evil if he's truly good. He has to have that predisposition in him. If he didn't, he would have broken the spell. Your friend mauled Skye. I'm afraid whatever part was human before, is long gone." He met my gaze. "I'm sorry."

As Alexander stood to leave, Bubba came downstairs. He followed him to the door to make sure it was still locked and then returned to the living room. "So not Boone."

"No," I grinned at him. "Not Boone."

The doorbell rang again.

Bubba stared down the hall. "Maybe he forgot his scarf?"

"Maybe. Do you want to go see?" I expected him to say no. He didn't like Boone, one bit.

He closed his eyes, then nodded. "Of course, whatever you need."

Nic watched as Bubba left the room to let Boone inside. "Are you sure Bubba's not under a compulsion spell?"

"I wouldn't do that." I tried to listen to see who was at the door. Then Boone and Bubba came into the living room.

"I can't stay long. I just wanted to check on you and grab that file." Boone's gaze scanned me, landing on the bandage on my shoulder. "How bad it the wound?"

"A scrape, but it stings." I admitted. "Have you found Aunt Franny or Will?"

"Actually, both are downtown waiting to chat with me. Your aunt is fit to be tied. If she hadn't been caught dragging Will out of the building, she might have made her way home and been able to make up an excuse." He flipped through the employment file. "Your friend on the other hand, he's a little less aware of what's going on. I've got a doctor coming, but I think he's not focusing on what's going on in this world."

"Will was Skye's boyfriend. He called himself Steve. He's mean, I've met him before." Lilac rubbed the leg of her jeans. Then she looked up at Boone. "Did he kill her?"

Boone focused on Lilac. "We're going to find out."

She wiped tears from her cheeks. "Thanks."

Boone stood and tucked the files under his shoulder. "Stay out of trouble for a few days while I figure this out, okay?"

"Hey, there's a second file there. It might explain a few more unsolved deaths in the area." I put away the idea of working on either one of my projects. Instead, I'd spend the weekend with Lilac and Bubba. Watching television, reading, playing games and eating. Maybe by Monday my shoulder wouldn't be screaming at me. "I'm not going anywhere all weekend. Unless someone gives me a trip to Hawaii or a massage."

"A second file?" Boone glared at me. "Where did that come from?"
"It just showed up. But I believe it's legit. And I get the Hawaii joke isn't funny. I'll stay inside. I want this over. I'm tired of looking over my shoulder all the time." I stood and moved toward the stairs. "I'm going to take a bath. I'll be in my room if anyone needs me."

I didn't have to wait for Monday to find out what had happened. Boone stopped by on Saturday night on his way home. Will, who must have been out from under Aunt Franny's spell by then had told Boone everything on Saturday morning. He even admitted to killing Skye, although he said he was possessed. He hadn't wanted to kill her, but Aunt Franny had been trying to point the blame on Uncle Arthur for the death. Will worked for his underground grifter team and had brought Skye into it for her talent.

Lilac rubbed her arms while Boone was talking. "Skye worried that he was going to try to pull me into the team. If he'd known about my talent, I might have been the one he killed."

I rubbed her back. "Will was confused. I'm just glad you're safe."

"Your aunt had a plan. We searched her house and found a whole wall covered with pictures and notes about the best way to take down your uncle and how to kill you." He handed over his phone and showed me a picture of me with a bunch of dart holes in my face. "Your aunt was convinced that if you died, your inheritance would go to her. I'm assuming she didn't mean the money that it appears you've already spent."

I smiled at him. Boone was trying but he had both feet planted firmly in reality. "Aunt Franny was distraught at losing her mother and the loss of what she considered her inheritance to me. I have plenty of examples where she tried to attack me."

Bubba spoke up. "The Ardronic security department filed all of them with your office. Eddie was in real danger from her aunt. That's why they assigned me to watch her full time."

"I've pulled the reports. With what we found in her mansion; I think your aunt is going to go away for a long time. Will's going to a mental health facility until we can determine if he's sane enough to go to trial. And I'm going home." Boone stood after finishing his coffee. "I'm beat. I'm glad you're all right, Eddie. Maybe I can take you to dinner this week. You deserve it for all you've been through."

Bubba was watching me closely so I smiled and nodded. "We'll see. I'm not quite up to my old self. Yet."

"I understand. Schedule some time to see your doctor. Wounds like that can go nasty fast if you don't watch them." He said his good-byes and headed out to the door. Bubba followed him.

As soon as Boone left the house, Nic called me. "So it's over?"

"I guess. Maybe Uncle Arthur wasn't as involved as we thought." I sipped my hot cocoa. I hadn't slept much Friday night, so I was trying to slow down on the caffeine today.

"He's still lying about something. Maybe it's this underground team. Maybe something else. But at least our aunt is out of our hair. Or she will be as soon as the trial is over, and she's locked up for good." Nic muttered something I couldn't hear over the phone. "Look, I've got to go. Eliza says to tell you that it's fine to hold off for a week or so before starting Clayborne Estates. If you need to."

"I'll see how Monday goes." I knew my uncle was lying to my brother about more than just the other con he was running. But that wasn't my story to tell. I really hoped that at least one of our remaining close relatives was still going to be around to be part of our family.

"Eddie? Is everything okay? I just lost connection with you." My brother asked as I turned off the Wi-Fi connection between the two of us in my head.

"Bubba and Lilac want to play a board game. I've got to go. Talk with you soon and tell Eliza hi." I wondered why Eliza was visiting Nic. I knew my new employer wanted more from my brother than just to check in with him to see how I was doing. But that was between Nic and Eliza and Esmeralda, Nic's absentee girlfriend.

I set down my phone and looked at Lilac. "Ready to play?"

"If you're sure you're feeling up to it." She pulled out the Scrabble game and started setting it up on the table. "You're not getting any pity points because you're not feeling well."

"You should give me all the pity points," Bubba added as he came inside from taking Dr. Dexter out. "I wasn't the strongest in English class."

As game night started, I pulled my hoodie closer. I was home and with people I cared about. We were safe here. Alexander Morgan had sent me flowers that morning telling me he was off to Paris and would check in when he returned to New Orleans.

All was good in my world. Except I really needed to hire more staff for my business. But that could wait for Monday.

Tonight was all about celebrating getting through another bad patch.

I had a feeling that these weren't behind us yet. I didn't know where the next shoe would drop from, but I knew it was coming. I could feel it.

Bubba was watching me. He pointed to my tile holder. "Eddie, are you ready? It's your turn."

～

A MEDIUM GIFT The fourth and final episode of Eddie Cayce's return home to New Orleans will arrive this winter.

What is Uncle Arthur hiding? And will Nic find out what his play is before the company goes under? With Aunt Franny in jail, is Eddie finally safe? Boone or Bubba?

Pre-order now - https://www.amazon.com/dp/B0C3T8NSYH? ref_=pe_3052080_276849420

～

The Haunted Life Cozy Mystery Series -
Book 1 – A MEDIUM FATE

I see ghosts, but I do my best to ignore them.

When Eddie Cayce turned home to New Orleans from her carefully built Seattle life, it's not just for her grandmother's funeral. She's home to stay. More to the point, now that she's broken it off with the almost fiancé and quit her corporate junior designer position over one too many trainings on how to run a copier, she has no reason to return.

With the money she'll receive in her inheritance, she can finally open the antique store she's always dreamed of – that as long as her ability to see ghosts stays dormant. In Seattle, her gift had dwindled down to seeing the occasional ghost during her morning runs in her Queen Anne neighborhood. But here? New Orleans is filled with the visitors, as her grandmother always called them. And now, they are finding Eddie and want to chat. Especially about the most recent murder.

The Haunted Life Cozy Mystery Series -
Book 2 - A MEDIUM HOMECOMING
Eddie Cayce has come home to New Orleans.
Good or bad, she's made her bed and now she has to sleep in it, like her mama always said. Even though she loves the town where she grew up, the gift she'd been given from her late grandmother was causing problems. Major problems.

Her aunt isn't talking to her. Eddie's talent is turned up to the equivalent of a million-watt light bulb. Walking down the street from her newly purchased antique store, she has to dodge questions and demands from the newly and not so dearly departed.

When her marketing associate, Tessa Hunt, dies unexpectedly, her ghost demands that Eddie find her killer, Eddie agrees to make some calls. Now if she could just keep Tessa from pushing her bad marketing tactics from beyond the grave.

All Eddie wants is a little piece and quiet so she can run her new business and find the perfect house. Is that too much to ask? Apparently, the answer is yes, at least in New Orleans.

LEGAL BITS

A Medium Life. The Haunted Life Mysteries by Lynn Cahoon

Made in the USA
Las Vegas, NV
27 June 2023

73976602R00066